REALM
OF DARKNESS

Other books by Cynthia Danielewski:

Dead of Night
After Dark
Edge of Night

REALM
OF DARKNESS

•

Cynthia
Danielewski

AVALON BOOKS
NEW YORK

Published by Thomas Bouregy & Co., Inc.
160 Madison Avenue, New York, NY 10016

Library of Congress Cataloging-in-Publication Data

Danielewski, Cynthia.
    Realm of darkness / Cynthia Danielewski.
        p. cm.
    ISBN 0-8034-9789-X (acid-free paper)
    I. Title.
    PS3604.A528R43 2006
    813'.6—dc22

                        2006003150

PRINTED IN THE UNITED STATES OF AMERICA
ON ACID-FREE PAPER
Y HADDON CRAFTSMEN, BLOOMSBURG, PENNSYLVANIA

For Jim

Chapter One

Rick Cory adjusted the straps on the main sail, his steps light and swift as he made his way around his sailboat. A quick glance up at the star-studded night sky assured him that conditions were perfect to take the boat out for a midnight cruise. The heat of the Florida sun had dissipated with dusk, and a soft summer breeze fanned his face as he walked around the vessel, permeating the air with the rich, fragrant scent of the Atlantic Ocean. After tightening one last tie to secure the sail, he headed toward the cooler that was sitting next to the wheel.

He had just opened a bottle of iced tea when the sound of footsteps on the dock alerted him. Turning in the direction of the sound, a welcoming smile came over his face as he saw his visitor. "Right on time," he murmured.

A slight laugh escaped from the woman who stepped cautiously onto the boat. "I try."

Rick reached out a hand to steady her as the boat

1

rocked under her weight. "I wasn't sure if you were going to be able to make it tonight since I didn't hear from you this afternoon."

She smiled apologetically. "I was going to call you, but I couldn't pick up a signal with my cell phone."

"It doesn't matter. The important thing is that you're here," he said, releasing his hold on her. He grabbed the double handle of the duffel bag she held. "Let me have this and I'll store it below."

"Thanks."

"Don't mention it. I have cold beverages in the cooler by the wheel. Help yourself to a drink," he invited, his voice carrying into the darkness as he made his way below deck.

The woman walked over to the cooler and lifted the lid, peering inside curiously. Reaching for a can of soda, she popped the top with a manicured fingernail. "It's a beautiful night for sailing," she casually remarked, raising her voice slightly to ensure that he heard her.

"The night's not the only thing that's beautiful," Rick replied as he came back on deck. His eyes took in her glistening blond hair and he reached out a hand to touch the glowing tresses. "Like living silk."

The woman backed away with a teasing glance. "Always the flatterer. So tell me, when do we get under way?"

Rick smiled, enjoying the light banter. "Any time you're ready."

"I've been ready for a long time."

"Then let's get the show on the road," he said as he walked over to the rope railing and began to remove the bumpers that protected the sides of the craft.

"Can I help you with that?" she asked, watching his actions.

"Sure. Store these in that chest under the seat," he instructed, handing her the bumpers and motioning with his chin to the small storage space located within the side bench.

The woman did as he requested before closing the top of the bench and clicking the lock. "All set."

"Great," Rick replied as he moved over to take the wheel. Reaching out, he turned the key in the ignition, listening with satisfaction as the motor coughed and came to life. He glanced over at the woman. "Sit down and relax. We'll put the sail up after we pass the jetty."

"All right."

Rick glanced over at his companion several times as he motored out beyond the rocks. The wind had begun to kick up slightly once they hit the open water, and he looked at her in concern. "Are you warm enough?"

"I'm fine. As you can see, I came prepared," she said, gesturing to the lightweight jacket that she wore. She looked at his bare arms. "Did you want me to get you something? A sweatshirt? A jacket?"

"No, I'm comfortable."

"Let me know if you change your mind."

"I will," Rick said, noticing the pure delight on her face. "You look like you're enjoying yourself."

She smiled slightly, making eye contact with him. "As I said earlier, I've been looking forward to tonight for a long time."

"I hope it's everything you expect. I'll do my best to make it memorable for you."

"I'm sure it will be."

Rick motored out to the desired spot before shutting down the engine. The other boats that were moored in the water were mere silhouettes in the night. "This should do it."

She looked around with interest, her eyes studying the boats in the distance that were illuminated by the full moon that shone above. "We're not going further out?"

"No need," Rick assured her as the boat rocked gently in the waves. The sound of the water lapping against the sides of the vessel was a soothing rhythm in the stillness of the night. "Don't worry. There's nobody on board those boats. We'll have all the privacy we need."

"Good. Privacy is exactly what I want."

"Great minds think alike," Rick teased, stepping away from the wheel. "I'm going to start putting up the sail. Want to help?" he asked, not waiting for her response as he moved swiftly and started untying the red sashes that secured the sail.

"Sure. But there's one thing that I have to do first."

"What's that?" he asked curiously, turning to look at her. His eyes widened at the sight that greeted him, and a single gunshot exploded into the night as his world went black.

Chapter Two

Brooke Jennings twisted restlessly on her bed as she tried to combat her latest bout of insomnia. Sleep seemed impossible. Watching television, counting sheep, and just letting her mind drift was having absolutely no effect in triggering whatever it was that would allow her mind to shut down and get some rest. With a sigh of resignation, she glanced at the clock on her nightstand. Five o'clock. Dawn would be breaking soon. The realization was a welcome relief.

Deciding that she had tossed and turned enough, she sat up and glanced around the room until she spotted her dog, Jake. The Great Dane's head lifted up from the floor, the blackness of his coat appearing as a shadow in the darkness. He looked over at her, as if sensing her gaze, and a single bark echoed through the house.

Brooke rose from the bed, and padded barefoot over to where the dog lay. Bending down, she fondled the dog's ears. "The nights keep getting longer, don't they boy. You would think that I would be used to them by now."

Reaching out, she lifted the dog's chin in her palm. "Give me a few minutes to get myself together, and I'll take you for a walk," she promised before rising and walking to the kitchen to get her first cup of coffee.

In the kitchen, she noticed that the timer on the coffee maker had already turned the unit on. Reaching into a cabinet for a mug, she poured a cup of the strong coffee, automatically adding cream and sugar.

As she stood by the kitchen window and stirred the hot beverage, her eyes were immediately drawn to the shimmering pool outside. The sun would be up soon, and with it would be the heat that accompanied the hot summer days that were so much a part of life in New Smyrna Beach, a residential beach town on the eastern shore of Florida. Taking Jake for a short walk on the beach a block away seemed like the perfect way to begin the day. Walking at dawn had always been one of her favorite pastimes, and she hoped it would take the edge off the restless feeling she was experiencing. A quick glance at the clock assured her that she still had time to beat the early morning walkers who inevitably found their way to the shoreline. Knowing her window of opportunity to avoid the crowd was small, she quickly finished her cup and poured another before she headed toward the shower.

Thirty minutes later, Brooke had Jake on his leash as they walked outside. Locking the door behind her, she headed toward the street. Her neighbor, Police Chief Mark Tanner had just stepped outside to retrieve his newspaper. He stopped as he saw her, waiting for her to reach his driveway.

"Morning," Mark mumbled, his voice still raspy from sleep. He ran a restless hand through his black hair, trying to bring some semblance of order to the short strands, while he blinked several times in an effort to bring her into focus. Unable to stifle a yawn, he hid it behind one hand as he studied her in the morning light, waiting for her to return the greeting.

Brooke smiled. "Good morning."

"Out a little early, aren't you?" he asked, noticing everything about her appearance, from the blond-highlighted hair that was freshly blown dry, to the slight hint of shadows under her eyes.

She shrugged. "I couldn't sleep, so I thought I would take Jake for a walk on the beach before the walkers and surfers arrived."

Mark nodded. He knew she suffered from insomnia, and he could sympathize with her. He suffered from the same affliction. "Want some company?"

"Sure," she said, unable to turn down his offer. "I can't promise that I'll be very good company, though," she felt compelled to warn.

"Don't worry. You won't have to entertain me. I'm comfortable with silence. Besides, the fresh air will probably do us both some good. I just need a few minutes to get myself together. Come inside and have a cup of coffee while I get dressed," he invited, turning and leading the way.

Brooke followed him inside his home, knowing he was being truthful about being comfortable with silence. They had spent many a night just enjoying each other's company. Sometimes it amazed her that their friendship had become so close in such a short period of time.

Mark was relatively new in town. While Brooke had lived in the area her whole life, and still lived in the same house she grew up in, Mark had moved down from New York less than a year ago, after his wife had died from leukemia. It had taken Brooke months of a casual friendship with him before he felt comfortable enough to share anything personal. She had discovered early on that he was a very private individual. He didn't believe in talking about his life. Past, present, or future. Which is why she had been totally stunned when he had shared the information about his wife. She remembered the exact moment he told her about his marriage.

They had been on her patio late one evening, enjoying the night air, when the conversation turned to relationships. She had recently broken up with someone after a two-year span, and found Mark an easy person to confide in. Afterward, he had opened up about his past. She found herself listening intently as he told her about his wife, and the long struggle she had with her disabling disease. The deep loss he felt was obvious in the way he spoke, and Brooke's heart had melted at the small show of vulnerability. A vulnerability totally out of character.

It was that night that marked the beginning for them. Their mutual trust and understanding cultivated a friendship that only seemed to get stronger with time. And it was a friendship that Brooke had come to count on.

Her thoughts were immediately drawn back to the present as they entered the small foyer of his house, and the frigid temperature of the air assaulted her. "It's freezing in here," she complained good-naturedly, shivering in the cold air-conditioned room. She absently ran her hands down her arms, trying to instill some warmth into her chilled bones.

Mark smiled. "That's only because you just came in from the oppressive heat outside."

Brooke laughed at his assessment. "It's the coolest part of the day right now."

"It's still too warm for my liking."

"It's only June. Wait until August comes," she warned, knowing that if he felt the weather was warm now, he would find August's temperatures unbearable.

"I'm already dreading it," he told her with an exaggerated shudder.

Brooke smiled at his response. "Why did you move to Florida if you don't like the heat?"

Mark shrugged and sobered slightly, the smile on his face no longer reaching his eyes. "Self-inflicted torture?"

"That's not a serious answer." She watched the transformation of his features.

"Who says?" he returned lightly before glancing at the watch on his wrist. "We'd better get a move on if we want to avoid the crowds down at the beach. Give me a few minutes and I'll be ready. Coffee's in the kitchen. Help yourself." He turned to walk down the short hallway to his bedroom.

Brooke watched him walk away, and a pang of guilt hit her as the reason for his expression finally clicked. She knew of the circumstances that had brought him here, and she could have kicked herself for saying anything that might bring up a painful past. "Mark?"

"Yeah?"

"I'm sorry if I said something to offend you."

Mark sighed and turned to face her, a smile of apology hovering on his lips. "Don't worry, you didn't."

"Are you sure?" she asked, needing to hear his reassurance. She had never deliberately hurt anyone in her life, and she didn't want to start with him. She valued their friendship too much.

"Positive," he replied, his eyes softening as he looked at her. "Help yourself to some coffee. I'll be back in a few."

Brooke watched him disappear into his bedroom before she turned toward the numerous photographs on his entertainment center. She didn't want coffee, she was more interested in his life, and the people that were close to him. Several pictures graced the shelves of the unit, and she couldn't contain her curiosity as she moved closer to them.

As she glanced at the photos, one picture in particular caught her attention. She reached for it, realizing that it was his wedding picture.

"That's Angela," Mark told her as he came up from behind.

Brooke jumped at the sound of his voice and quickly turned, almost dropping the photograph. He had come up so quietly that she had failed to hear him. "You startled me."

"Sorry," his smile not hiding the pain that flashed briefly in his eyes as he studied the photograph.

"Your wife was beautiful," she told him sincerely, carefully placing the photograph back on the shelf.

"Yes, she was," he agreed, offering her another smile before glancing down at her empty hands. "You didn't want any coffee?"

"No, thanks. I had enough before I left the house. But you go ahead and have some."

Mark shook his head. "That's already the second pot this morning. I can wait until we get back."

Brooke looked at him in surprise. "The second pot? I thought you had just gotten up."

Mark shrugged. "It's been one of those mornings."

"I've had a few of those myself. Are you sure that you don't want another cup before we go?"

"No. I'm good."

"Then maybe we should head out. Jake's getting restless," she said, motioning to the dog who was sniffing the bottom of the door and hitting it with his paw.

Mark glanced at the dog and grinned at his antics. "Let me get my cell phone and we'll hit the road."

"Do you take the phone with you wherever you go?" she asked curiously, knowing that they probably wouldn't be gone long enough for him to need it.

"Do you think I would go anywhere in this crime-ridden neighborhood without it?" he mocked as he pocketed his keys and ushered her out the door.

"Are you making fun of our small town?"

"Who me? Never. If there's no crime here, who am I to complain? It looks great on my record."

She smiled at his response and took a deep breath of the salty sea air, revering in the kaleidoscope of colors that painted the sky as the sun rose over the ocean. "I love this time of day."

"Mm," Mark murmured as he locked the door and they started to walk down the driveway. He absently glanced at the other houses nestled in the quiet neighborhood, noting there was no sign of life in the early morning hour. The sight didn't surprise him. School was out for the summer, and it was still too early for people to begin leaving for work. "So tell me, why are you up so early?"

"I couldn't sleep."

"Any particular reason?"

"Bad genes?"

"Insomnia's not hereditary."

She glanced over at him. "You suffer from the same affliction. You know how the nights get sometimes."

"Yeah, I do. But I have a general idea of what causes mine. You don't. I've seen you out walking a lot lately in the morning."

She shrugged off the observation as being of no importance. "I love walking on the beach at this time of day."

"Uh huh," he murmured dryly.

She laughed. "I do. Don't you?"

"There is a certain amount of appeal to it. But somehow you don't strike me as the type to get up early just to appreciate the sunrise."

"That goes to show just how much you know about me," she teased.

"I know you well enough to know that during the school year, you appear to move in slow motion in the morning," he replied, making a reference to her job as a teacher at the local elementary school.

"True," she acknowledged, unable to deny his statement. She openly admitted that her energy level in the morning was marginal at best. "But then, I'm on my way to work. Who rushes to get to their job?"

Mark shook his head at her response, a smile hovering on his lips. "Try another excuse. I know for a fact that you love your job."

"Yeah, I do," she confessed without hesitation. She did love her work, and she had known Mark long enough to realize that he would have caught on to the fact.

Mark turned to look at her. His eyes took in the slight pallor of her skin that was noticeable beneath her tan, as well as the dark circles beneath her eyes. It had been his concern upon seeing just how tired she looked that had prompted him to accompany her on the walk.

When he had moved to the little town almost a year ago, he had basically done it to start a new life. He was tired of dealing with the jaded, cynical people of New York, and welcomed the change to what he considered oblivion. He wanted to forget his problems, immerse himself in his work. He hadn't counted on moving to a place where true crime was practically non-existent. Petty crime was the norm here, but then again, petty crime was everywhere. But it was pretty hard to lose yourself in it. Meeting his quiet neighbor had given him a distraction from facing his own problems. Brooke was a second-grade schoolteacher who seemed to embody small-town life. She had no great expectations, and she was content to just live her life as she saw fit. She was careful about prying into his private life, so he felt safe in the casual socialization they had. But their friendship had also opened up feelings of concern for her well-being.

"You're not going to tell me what's bothering you and keeping you up at night?" he persisted as they crossed the road and walked toward the palm trees clustered around the dunes.

"It's nothing," she assured him as they neared their destination and she heard the gentle roar of the ocean.

"So that's why you're walking your dog on the beach even though there are signs posted all around that no dogs are allowed."

"Are you going to arrest me?"

"I should at least issue a summons," he told her lightheartedly.

She smiled. "But you won't."

"Not if you tell me what's keeping you up at night."

Brooke stopped walking as they came to the small boardwalk that led to the beach. Her eyes met Mark's briefly before she bent down to release the dog's leash. Watching Jake as he took off toward the water, she said, "There's nothing to tell. I mean, I'm tired when I go to bed at night, but sleep just doesn't come."

"Have you seen a doctor?"

"Yeah. He said not to worry. It'll pass."

Mark shot her a knowing look. "Did he actually say that? Or is that just your interpretation?"

Brooke was about to respond to his cryptic question when Jake's barking interrupted them. They both turned in his direction. Brooke started to call the dog when Mark muttered a single distinct curse and took off toward the water at a dead run. Brooke watched him go, trying to see what had caused his reaction, when she noticed the dark object floating in the surf. Her curiosity peaked, she quickly followed him.

She was out of breath when she reached the shoreline, and she stood there helplessly as Mark waded into the sea. Grabbing the dog's collar, she hunched down next to him and watched as Mark picked up the object and dragged it to shore. She shielded her eyes from the harsh glare of the sun as she tried to see what he had.

Mark turned to look at her and nodded to his cell phone that he had dropped on the sand. "Call nine-one-one and tell them to get a car out here now," he ordered grimly, his face a mask of pure steel.

"Why?" Brooke asked, unable to get a clear view of what he was towing to the water's edge.

"Just do it!"

Brooke responded to the urgency of his words and did as he requested before placing the phone back on the sand. Issuing a firm order to the dog to stay put, she walked closer to where Mark stood. Shock ripped through her as she caught her first glimpse of the body that he dragged to shore.

Chapter Three

Mark laid the body of the man on the beach and automatically reached out to check for a pulse. He cursed under his breath when he failed to locate it. His eyes raked over the man, noticing the bullet hole on the shirt near his heart and the obvious bloodstains on his clothing.

Turning to face the ocean, he shielded his eyes from the sun's glare as he looked out beyond the breakers for any boats, anything that would give him a clue as to what had happened. But other than a few dolphins swimming in the distance, he couldn't locate anything on the horizon. The only other activity belonged to the seagulls and pelicans diving for food.

"Is he dead?" Brooke asked tentatively as she looked at the lifeless form. She felt strangely lightheaded, and the breeze blowing in from the ocean was soothing against her clammy flesh as she waited for Mark's answer. She concentrated on breathing normally as she studied the man lying on the beach, her eyes searching for any movement, any sign of life.

Mark stood up and pushed a weary hand through his hair. "Yeah," he said as he turned to her. His brow furrowed in concern at the paleness of her features. "Are you all right? You look as if you're about to pass out."

Brooke took in a shaky breath. "I know him."

"What did you say?"

"I know this man."

Mark was stunned by her words. "Who is he?" he demanded, his eyes staying glued to her face as he waited for her response.

"Rick Cory," she said, her voice barely above a whisper. She looked up at Mark with haunted eyes. "I was engaged to him."

Mark stared at her in disbelief. "This is the guy you told me about? The one you broke the engagement with?"

"Yes."

Mark looked down at the victim. "When was the last time you saw him?"

"A couple of weeks ago. I ran into him at the bank."

Mark was surprised that she didn't mention anything to him at the time. She usually shared things like that with him. "Was he all right when you saw him?"

"All right? What do you mean?"

"Did he appear to be acting normally? Was he displaying any behavior that you thought was strange?"

Brooke's mind went back to the day she had seen Rick. Try as she might, she couldn't recall anything out of the ordinary about Rick's mannerisms. Though their conversation had been brief, he behaved the same way he always had around her. Like a perfect gentleman. "He seemed fine."

"Do you know of anybody who wanted to see him dead?" he asked bluntly, instantly regretting the question when she paled.

"No," she replied softly, trying to come to terms with seeing Rick's body lying lifeless on the sand. "Was he shot?"

"What?" Mark asked, watching her closely. She was acting strangely out of character, and he began to worry that seeing the body might have been too much for her. He had her pictured as an old-fashioned schoolteacher, someone who probably never saw a violent act in her life. Someone who was so sheltered from life's harsh realities that they couldn't begin to imagine the atrocities that some people experienced every day of their lives. He knew seeing the body had to have a deep effect on her, especially since she knew the victim. Since she had a relationship with the victim.

Brooke motioned to Rick Cory's body. "Was he shot?" she repeated, her eyes straying to Rick's shirt, noticing the dark stains on the material that resembled blood, and the ragged hole in the cloth.

"Yes," Mark confirmed. He studied her in silence, watching the myriad of emotions that crossed her facial features, wondering what she was thinking.

Brooke didn't notice his speculative gaze. She closed her eyes in despair at hearing him confirm what she already suspected, and she swayed slightly on her feet.

Alarmed, Mark quickly moved to catch her forearms to keep her from falling. "Hey. Why don't you sit down before you fall down," he told her gently as he tried to ease her onto the sand.

"I'm all right," she assured him.

"Right," he muttered in disbelief. Out of the corner of his eye, he caught sight of the flashing lights of the emergency vehicles arriving on the scene. He spared them only a passing glance before focusing back on Brooke. "Just sit down for a minute and take some deep breaths."

"Really, I'm okay."

"Are you sure?"

"Yes," she said, following his advice and taking a deep breath, forcing herself to take control of her turbulent emotions.

Mark cast another quick look at the officers who had arrived. "I have to go and talk to them," he said, motioning with his chin to the people who were beginning to surround the body. He didn't want to leave her in the state she was in, but his job beckoned.

"Of course."

"Will you be all right?" he asked, his eyes studying her intensely. He needed some sort of assurance from her that she would be okay, something other than words. He needed to know that it was safe to leave her alone. He had been on the police force long enough to realize that people reacted differently to seeing death, but her demeanor really threw him. He hadn't expected her to fall apart. All of his protective instincts came to the forefront at her obvious show of vulnerability.

"I'll be fine."

Mark looked down at her, reluctant to leave her side.

"Do you think you can manage to get home okay?" he asked gently, his tone of voice deliberately trying to soothe her, to give her some sort of strength.

"Home?"

"Yeah. I think it would be a good idea for you to leave the area. There'll be more people coming shortly. This place is going to be a mob scene in no time. There's no reason for you to hang around."

"I'll—" She was interrupted by additional sirens piercing the air.

Mark looked over to where more emergency vehicles were in the process of parking before bringing his attention back to Brooke. "You were going to say . . ." he prompted, torn between concern for her well-being and the need to begin his investigation.

Brooke ran a shaking hand over her eyes and tried once more to get a grip on her emotions. "I'll go back to the house."

"It's for the best."

She nodded and looked around until she spotted her dog. "Let me call Jake," she said, snapping her fingers once to bring the dog to her side. She attached the leash to the dog's collar, feeling the heat reflected from the blackness of his coat. The warmth was oddly comforting.

"Let me get someone to walk with you."

"That's not necessary."

"Brooke . . ." he began, not comfortable with letting her leave by herself in the condition she was in. He would feel better if a uniformed officer escorted her back to her house and stayed with her, at least until he was able to get there.

"Really, I'm okay."

Mark hesitated a moment longer before nodding. "I'll come by as soon as I'm through here."

"Okay."

"Are you sure you're all right?" he asked, feeling compelled to ask the question one final time.

"Yeah. I'll be fine," she assured him softly before turning and slowly walking away.

Mark stared after her until he was satisfied that she would be able to get home with no problems before turning in the direction of the approaching officers. He walked over to the criminalist who had begun snapping pictures of the deceased. "Make sure you get every angle of the body."

Megan Smith looked up at him with a slight grin and absently flicked her blond hair over her shoulder. "You can trust me."

Mark smiled at the confidence in her voice, and the easy manner she had about her. "I'm counting on it," he told her, realizing as he spoke just how much truth was in the simple statement. He did count on Megan. The dedication she had to her job, the wealth of knowledge she had of forensics, and the charm that was such an innate part of her character made it easy to do so. She was a valued colleague as well as a friend, and he couldn't help but admire her. Especially when he considered the circumstances that drove her in her chosen career. Megan's decision to join the police department had been motivated by her mother being taken at knifepoint in a convenience store holdup. The woman had been lucky and survived the ordeal, but the suspect had walked away scot-free due to a lack of evidence. And now, Megan made it her mission in life to ensure that would never happen to another victim, and Mark respected her for her commitment.

As he stood there quietly, observing Megan, he heard someone clearing their throat. Turning, he was surprised to find Detective Walt Tyler walking toward him.

"Hey," Walt greeted, rubbing a tired hand across his eyes. He reached up to remove his baseball cap, his hand running through his wheat-colored hair before adjusting the cap back on his head, and pulling the bill low over his eyes to keep the sun out.

"Hi," Mark replied, his eyebrows raised slightly at Walt's appearance on the beach. "What are you doing here? I thought you took the week off."

Walt shrugged. "That was the plan. I was supposed to be on a one o'clock flight to California today."

"What happened?"

"I left something at my desk yesterday and stopped by the station this morning to get it when your call came through. I thought I would come and see what the commotion was about."

Mark smiled at Walt's words. "The station's in an uproar, huh?"

"That's putting it mildly," Walt said as he studied the deceased. "You would think that there had never been a murder in this town."

Mark lifted one shoulder expressively. "There hasn't been for quite a while."

"Yeah, well, this will give everybody a chance to practice their investigation skills," Walt said matter-of-factly as he walked slowly around the body, his eyes searching the victim. "I have to tell you, I never expected to see this here. Daytona maybe, but not here."

"I know what you mean," Mark said. Walt had moved to the area from Los Angeles about six months ago and had struck up an instant friendship with Mark, the two of them finding a common bond that came from working homicide in big cities. Mark knew that to the outside world, Walt gave the impression of being a laid-back Californian, more concerned about maintaining his tan than in solving any cases. But Mark had seen firsthand just how deep was Walt's dedication to the job. He had seen the commendations in his file. He knew of his track record in solving homicides. The baseball cap that he always seemed to be wearing was just a cover–up, a disguise masking the true professional.

"Any ideas on where the guy came from?" Walt asked.

"At a guess, he either fell or was pushed off a boat. I do have an idea of his identity, though."

"Already? Was he carrying ID?"

"No. I was out walking with my neighbor when we stumbled across him. She was able to identify him. His name is Rick Cory."

"Which neighbor were you walking with?"

"Brooke Jennings."

"The schoolteacher?"

"Yeah."

Walt's forehead creased in a frown. "How did she know him?"

"She used to be engaged to him."

Walt gave a soft whistle. "Seeing the body must have been a shock for her."

Mark grunted. "That's putting it mildly."

"Did you question her yet?"

"No. I sent her home. She really wasn't in any condition to answer questions. I think she needs some time to come to terms with seeing the body."

"Anybody would."

Mark sighed. "Ain't that the truth. I'm going to head over to her house after we're through here to check on her. If she's feeling up to it, I'll see if I can find out anything on our victim."

"Sounds good," Walt replied, his thoughts going back to the crime scene. He turned, his eyes scanning the beach and the pier in the distance. "Do you think there's a chance that someone dumped the body from the pier?"

"I think it's doubtful. I'm more inclined to believe that a boat was somehow involved. You know as well as I do that the pier usually has foot traffic at night. Especially in the summer months. Between the teenagers that hang out and the old-timers that like to shrimp at night, I think it would be hard for someone to ditch the body without being noticed."

"We don't know how long he could have been drifting."

Mark shrugged. "By a guess, he couldn't have been in the water for too long. Maybe five or six hours. There's not enough deterioration to his body to indicate a longer span."

Walt bent down to inspect the forearm of the victim. "I guess we're lucky that the sharks didn't get him. They usually come in to feed at dawn."

Mark noticed the deep concentration on Walt's face as he examined something that had caught his attention. "What do you see?"

"Hair."

"What?"

"Hair. Tangled in the strap of his watch," Walt said as he pointed to the object in question.

Mark looked down at the wet strand. It was a long, blond strand. "It could belong to his wife or girlfriend."

"It could."

"Or it could belong to the killer."

"It's possible," Walt agreed as he stood and stretched his legs.

"We'll have to see what comes up after we get it analyzed," Mark said, glancing over and catching sight of Megan as she spoke to another criminalist. "Megan," he called, motioning for her to come over.

Megan looked at Mark to acknowledge that she had heard him, and after finishing her conversation with the other criminalist, she carefully made her way over to Mark and Walt. "Did you find something?" she asked, her eyes automatically shifting to the body.

"There's a strand of hair tangled in the guy's watch," Walt replied.

Megan bent down to examine the potential piece of evidence. "I see it," she assured him, reaching for her camera to photograph the position of the evidence before she began the task of collecting it.

"How long do you think it'll take to get the forensics report?" Walt asked her, watching as she painstakingly untangled the piece of hair from the watch, being careful not to break the strand.

Megan looked up from her task, her face a mask of pure concentration. "It shouldn't take long to get. Hopefully we'll have it by tonight."

Walt nodded slightly. "Great."

"I'll make sure this gets priority," she promised, going back to the job at hand.

"We appreciate that," Walt said before turning to Mark. "How did you find the body?"

Mark rubbed a hand across the tense muscles of his neck. "Floating in the waves. He wasn't that far out. Eventually, he would have washed up on shore. I'm just glad that the beach was empty at the time. I would have hated for some unsuspecting swimmer to run across him."

"Finding something like that would be enough to give anyone cardiac arrest."

"You got that right," Mark replied, falling silent as the coroner's van arrived at the scene. He took a couple of steps back as the coroner walked over to examine the body, watching the clinical detachment that the man displayed. He knew that the man's attitude wasn't one of callousness, but rather it was a defense mechanism that came with years of experience in dealing with death. It was a skill that most people in law enforcement learned early on. The hard fact was that you couldn't perform your job properly if you let emotions get in the way.

Out of respect for the situation, Mark watched quietly while the body of the victim was lifted into a black body bag and then loaded into the cargo area of the vehicle. He waited until the van drove away before turning to Walt. "You feel up to combing the beach?"

Walt glanced at him. "Do you think we'll find anything?"

"I honestly don't know. It's worth a shot," Mark said,

knowing that if there was any physical evidence, there was a strong possibility that it would eventually wash up on shore.

"I'm game."

"Why don't we split up," Mark suggested. "We'll make better time that way."

"Sounds good." Walt adjusted his sunglasses. "I'll meet you back here in a little bit."

A short time later, Mark was back at the spot where the body had been discovered. He was in the process of going over some pieces of evidence with the criminalists, when Walt walked over.

"Find anything?" Walt asked.

Mark turned. "Yeah, and it looks like it belongs to our floater."

"What is it?"

Mark reached down for the clear plastic bag that rested in the small black case the technicians were using to gather evidence. "This," he said, holding the item up.

Walt frowned. "A prescription bottle?"

"Yeah. The name on the label is a little smeared from being in the water, but it's still legible."

Walt reached for the plastic bag and squinted in an attempt to read the label. "Rick Cory," he said, reading the name aloud.

"The same name Brooke gave as an identity. I already have someone running a background check on him," Mark said.

"Where did you find the bottle?"

"Not too far away from where I noticed the body. It's

possible the guy had the bottle in his pocket. There are still pills inside. Maybe he needed to keep them close by in case of an emergency."

"What kind of pills are they? Could you tell?"

"Nitroglycerine."

"My old man carries those for his heart," Walt said.

"That's what they're for," Mark said distractedly as he looked out over the ocean.

Walt followed his gaze. "Do you see something?"

"No, I was just thinking about the ocean's conditions. The water's rough today, and the currents are strong. I doubt that much else will wash up on the beach."

"I agree."

"I put out a bulletin to the other jurisdictions to keep an eye out for anything suspicious. But to be honest, with the amount of beach-goers during this time of year, I'm not holding out much hope that any additional evidence is going to turn up. Not unless it's substantial and stands out."

Walt nodded, and turned toward the small group of people beginning to gather on the path to the beach. "It didn't take too long for people to get wind of this."

Mark shrugged, watching the small crowd. "This is big news. I'm surprised that it took as long as it did for people to come and check out what was going on. We should consider ourselves lucky that we had at least some time without any distractions to go over the area. If this had happened any later in the day, the integrity of any evidence would have been compromised." He glanced at his watch. "If you don't get a move on, you're going to miss your plane."

Walt adjusted the rim of his baseball cap before casually saying, "I've been thinking. Maybe now wouldn't be a good time to leave."

Mark looked over at him with a slight smile. "Too much excitement to pass up?" he asked, gesturing to the technicians that were still combing the area for evidence.

Walt smiled. "It has been a little slow around here lately."

"That it has," Mark agreed, knowing that Walt like himself was having difficulty adjusting to small-town life and the lack of cases that required the skills they had both taken so long to hone.

"It'll be interesting to see where all of this leads."

"If you're serious about canceling your vacation, I wouldn't turn down the help."

"I'm serious. I can go to California another time."

"Are you sure?" Mark asked, not wanting to pressure Walt.

"Yeah, I'm sure."

"What about your wife?"

Walt looked over at him with a frown. "What about her?"

"Don't you think you should check with her before you start changing your plans? I thought she was looking forward to getting away."

"She was just excited about taking some time off of work. I don't think she'll care whether or not she goes to California. She'll be just as happy spending her days on the beach."

Mark looked at him doubtfully. "I hope you're right about that."

"Trust me."

Mark laughed. "It's your funeral. If you're serious, let's see if we can get everything wrapped up here before the crowd gets any larger."

"You got it."

Chapter Four

It was a couple of hours later before Mark found himself knocking on Brooke's door. He shifted impatiently while he waited for her to answer, and ran a tired hand across the back of his neck, kneading his tense muscles.

As he stood there waiting, he thought about how quickly the stretch of beach where the body had been discovered had become a mob scene, the news vans pulling up just as they were finishing their search. He had hoped to get out of the area before they arrived. The press had the ability to turn any news story into a feeding frenzy, and dealing with them was the one thing he hated about his job. It was the one thing that he didn't have the patience for. He had run into too many problems from inaccurate reporting. Too many instances where the press wasn't truthful with the facts. He was under no illusions where reporters were concerned. He knew biased reporting was common, and sensationalism sold stories. He didn't want the details of this particular investigation to become fodder for the news organizations. He didn't want the investigation to be jeopardized in any way. He was lost in his own thoughts, thinking of the people he could call in favors to in an effort to keep the case as close to the police as possible, when Brooke answered the door.

"Mark."

Mark smiled slightly and leaned a shoulder against the door frame. "Hi." His eyes searched her face, noticing that the stress from that morning was still evident in her features.

"Hi. How did everything go down at the beach?" she asked, wondering if he had found out anything about Rick's murder.

"About how I expected," he replied before asking the question that was uppermost in his mind. "How are you doing? You really had me worried this morning."

"I'm sorry about that."

"You don't have to apologize."

"I usually do better in a crisis," she assured him.

"I know. That's one of the reasons I'm so concerned."

She grimaced self-consciously. "Thank you, but you don't have to be. As you can see, I'm fine."

"I'm glad you're feeling better," he said, though he wasn't sure if he believed her. Her words sounded a little hollow. Wanting to spend some time with her to assure himself that she was truly all right, he motioned to the open doorway. "Would you mind if I came in for a while?"

"Of course not," she said, surprised that he even thought he had to ask. She stepped back to allow him to enter the house. "I didn't expect to see you so soon. I thought you would have been tied up down at the beach."

Mark shrugged. "The crime scene, if you could call it that, was pretty clean."

"Is that good or bad?"

"Neither. It just means that we don't have a lot to go on."

"I was afraid you would say that."

"I wish I had better news for you. I know seeing the body had to be a shock."

Brooke ran an agitated hand through her hair. "It was."

Mark looked at her, studying her face in the late morning light. She was too pale. He didn't like it. "Do you feel up to talking?"

"You mean about Rick?"

"Yeah. I was hoping you would be able to tell me a little bit about him. It might help fit together the pieces of what happened."

"I don't know if I could tell you anything that would help."

"Right now, anything you could tell me would be helpful."

She nodded in understanding. "Of course. I'll tell you what I know."

"I appreciate that."

"Before we start, can I get you a cold drink?" she asked, knowing that he had been down at the beach for hours and was probably ready for a cool drink.

"Please."

"I'll be right back."

"Okay," Mark replied, watching as she left the room.

He heard her moving around in the kitchen for about a minute before she returned, carrying a tray.

"Here we go," she said.

Mark automatically reached out to take the tray from her hands. "I got it," he said, placing it on the coffee table.

"Thanks."

"Why don't you sit down and relax? You look as if you're about to fall off your feet."

Brooke gave a slight laugh, but it contained no humor. "It shows?"

Mark shrugged. "Any way you look at it, it's been a rough morning."

"I know." She took a seat next to him, and reached for the plastic pitcher on the tray. Pouring out two glasses of iced tea, she handed him one.

"Thanks," Mark said. He took a sip before placing the glass on a coaster on the coffee table. "Are you sure you're feeling up to this?"

"Right now, I'm not even sure of my own name."

"Well, just tell me what you can. If you need to stop, we will. We can always continue the conversation when you're feeling better."

She nodded and shot him a grateful look. Taking a deep breath, she asked, "What did you want to know?"

"Everything," he replied without hesitation. "But for starters, can you tell me if there's anyone in Rick's life that we should contact?"

"There's no one. Rick's parents died several years back, and as far as I know, he wasn't dating anybody seriously."

"Any brothers or sisters?"

"No."

Mark nodded slightly and took another sip of his drink. "That's tough being all alone."

Brooke was silent for a moment before saying, "Rick wasn't alone. He was a great guy. He had lots of friends."

"You had dated him for two years, right?"

"Yes. I met him through one of my co-workers. Sharon Millstone. She had a party for her brother, Evan, when he made partner in the law firm he worked at."

"How did they know Rick?"

"Rick worked as an attorney at the same law firm."

Mark thought of his past conversations with Brooke. "I think I remember you telling me that your fiancé was an attorney."

"He was a friend of Sharon's brother."

"You guys hit it off right away, didn't you?"

"We did. Rick had a great sense of humor," she said as she recalled their time together.

Mark noticed the glimmer of tears in her eyes. "If this is too painful to talk about . . ." He gave her the opening to end the discussion if she needed it.

Brooke took a shaky breath. "No, I'm fine."

"Are you sure?"

"Yeah."

"Let me know if you need to stop."

"I will." She paused for just a moment to regain her composure. "Anyway, like I said, Rick and I hit it off right away. We had a lot in common. We liked the same books, the same type of movies, even the same types of food. Everything seemed to be going along perfectly. Until we started planning our future together."

Mark turned sideways on the sofa so he could see her better. "You never actually told me what it was that caused your breakup."

"Didn't I?"

"No. You just said that you both came to realize that you wanted different things in life."

She paused for another moment as she called to mind the things she had told Mark on that night that seemed so long ago. "I'm sorry. I thought I had mentioned to you the true reason for our breakup. I wanted children and Rick didn't."

Mark leaned back against the sofa as he digested her words. "That's a hard thing to overcome," he said sympathetically, knowing of a few marriages that had broken up because of that very thing.

"Without someone compromising, it's impossible to overcome."

"I know," he admitted, feeling as if he should say something else, but not knowing what else to say. He knew the topic of children could be a turning point in any relationship. It was just a fact of life.

She lifted a shoulder slightly in a shrug. "If things aren't right, you can't force them. I'm grateful that Rick was honest with me. I can think of nothing worse than finding out something of that magnitude after the vows."

"I agree," Mark said, falling silent, wanting to give her the opportunity to talk if she needed to. But when she didn't say anything else, he prompted, "What else can you tell me about Rick? Did he have any enemies that you were aware of? Anybody that would want to hurt him?" he asked gently, trying to feel his way around the conversation. He didn't want to say something to upset her, but he needed information that would help him find out who murdered Rick Cory.

"Rick was an attorney. He made his share of adversaries in the courtroom," she said.

"What type of law did he practice?"

"Criminal. He was a defense attorney. I recently heard that he had left the law firm he was working for and opened his own practice. I can give you the name of his secretary in case you want to talk to her. It's Marissa James. She was with him at the other firm. From my understanding, she left her job so that she could continue to work for him."

"It sounds like she had a strong sense of loyalty toward him."

"I'm sure he paid her well. Rick always did everything first class," she said, pausing for a moment before continuing. "Do you mind if I ask you something?"

Mark looked at her in surprise. "Of course I don't mind. What do you want to know?"

"I wanted to ask if you had any theories on how Rick could have ended up in the water."

"At a guess, he fell off a boat. Or he was pushed."

Brooke's eyes shot up to meet Mark's. "Rick owns a sailboat."

Mark stilled at her words. "Where does he keep it docked?"

"Ponce Inlet Marina."

Mark reached for his cell phone as soon as the words left her mouth and dialed the station. He hung up a couple of minutes later. "They're going to send a couple of cars out to the location to check out the boat."

Brooke stared at him for a long moment before saying, "I'm sorry I didn't think to mention the fact earlier."

"Don't worry about it."

"Do you think someone murdered Rick on board his own boat?"

"To be honest, I don't know. Right now, we're not even sure of exactly what happened. The murder could have been self-defense, manslaughter, premeditated, or just an accident where someone used poor judgment. All of the options are currently open. We need more details in order to narrow it down."

She thought about his words. "I don't think it was an accident," she said distractedly.

"What wasn't?"

"Rick's death."

"No, it doesn't look like it was, but like I said, we really don't have enough information to go on just yet."

"Rick valued his privacy. Anybody he went sailing with would have been a trusted friend."

"You don't think he could have taken a client out on the water with him? Maybe someone who had a grudge against him? You said he was a defense attorney. Maybe one of his clients wasn't happy with their representation."

Brooke shook her head. "Rick cherished his boat. It was his outlet for relaxation. I've never known him to mix business with pleasure. At least not when it came to sailing."

"You sound very sure of that."

"I spent two years of my life with the man."

"If what you're saying is true, there's still the possibility that his death could have been an accident."

"No. He was a staunch believer in gun control. There was no way he would have owned a gun."

"Nobody's saying the gun was his."

"But he wouldn't have even let someone carry one onto the boat," she replied adamantly.

"Why do you say that?"

She looked over at him. "You remember before when I told you that Rick didn't want children?"

"Yeah?"

"He had his own reasons for that."

"What were they?"

"There's something I didn't mention earlier. Rick was married before, and he had a son."

"So?" Mark questioned, not understanding the relevance of the statement.

"His son was killed by a gun. Rick was the intended target."

Chapter Five

Mark stared at her, stunned. "What did you just say?" He wondered if he had heard her right.

"Rick's son was killed by a gun."

"And he was the intended target?"

"Yes," she replied as she took a sip of her drink. The coldness of the glass felt soothing against her flesh and she leaned back into the sofa as she tried to think of the best way to tell him about what she knew of the situation.

When she sat in silence for a moment too long, Mark warned, "Brooke, you can't just make a statement like that and not elaborate."

"I know," she acknowledged softly. "I'm not avoiding talking. I'm trying to think of the best way to start."

"The best place to start is at the beginning," he prompted gently.

She nodded, her finger tracing the rim of her glass while she gathered her thoughts.

"I had told you that Rick was a defense attorney."

"Yes."

"Well with that, you're bound to run into a fair share of people that aren't always happy with the outcome of a case. Whether it be a client or a victim, someone isn't going to be happy with the result of a court case."

"That goes with the territory."

"Yes it does," she agreed. "Except in this particular instance, Rick was defending a man accused of manslaughter. Emotions were running high."

"Manslaughter? What were the grounds?"

"A hit and run. It happened late at night on an unlit street. Rick's client claimed that he never saw the man changing the flat tire on the side of the road."

"Did the evidence support the claim?"

"To be honest, I'm not sure. But the victim had enough alcohol in his blood to label him as legally intoxicated. There was enough doubt raised as to whether he contributed to his own death by stumbling in front of the car."

"What was the defense for the guy not to stop?" Mark asked curiously.

"There was construction on the road. He claimed he thought he hit one of the orange road cones. Anyway, to make a long story short, the victim's widow went off the deep end and blamed Rick for getting the guy off scot-free. After the trial was over, she managed to get hold of a gun and fired at Rick outside a restaurant."

"She stalked him?"

Brooke lifted a shoulder expressively. "In a nutshell. Rick had his teenage son with him at the time. The bullet ricocheted off of the restaurant building and hit Rick's son, Jason. By the time they got him to the hospital, he was dead. Rick had a heart attack the same night."

Mark was silent for a moment before saying, "The stress of dealing with something of that magnitude is excessive. If he had any heart problems to begin with, that incident was probably the final trigger."

"I know."

"We found a prescription bottle of nitroglycerine on the beach this morning with Rick's name on it," Mark admitted.

"After that night, he always carried them, just in case."

"What happened to the woman responsible for the shooting?"

Brooke took another sip of her drink before responding. "She's serving a life sentence."

"What's her name?" Mark asked, wanting to run a full background check on the couple to see if there was anyone in the shadows who might have a motive for killing Rick Cory.

"Ellen Manning. Her husband was Arthur Manning."

Mark made a mental note of the names. "Just out of curiosity, what was the woman's defense?"

"At the time, she claimed that she didn't mean to kill anyone. That she was just trying to scare Rick. To have him feel the same sense of fear she was sure that her husband felt the night he was hit by the car," she replied, her disgust over the woman's defense evident in her voice.

"Almost everybody will find some justification or excuse for their actions," Mark said.

"I know. And Rick knew that better than anyone. But he never got over the death of his son."

"And Rick's wife?"

"Randy? To be honest, I don't know too much about her. They divorced years ago, and Rick had full custody of his son."

"Do you have any idea of where she's living?" Mark asked, knowing that there was always that possibility that the woman had blamed Rick for their son's death and had sought some sort of revenge.

"She was originally from Tallahassee. I think she moved back there after their divorce, but I'm not sure."

Mark was silent for a moment as he considered her information. "Maybe something will come up in the trace we're running."

"I hope so."

"I appreciate everything you've been able to tell me. At least I have some idea of where to start looking for answers."

Her eyes met his. "I want to help in any way I can."

"I know you do. I'll let you know if I have any more questions."

She nodded slightly, catching sight of his now empty glass. "Can I pour you another drink?"

"No thanks." He cast a quick glance at his watch and stood up. "I should be going. I have to get down to the police station. I'm afraid I left things hanging when I came over here. Will you be all right on your own?"

"Yes."

Mark's eyes searched hers. "Are you sure?"

"Yeah." She rose from her chair. "Thanks again for coming to check on me."

"Don't mention it."

"I'll walk you out."

"Thanks," he said, walking beside her through the

house. As they arrived at the front door, he turned. "Do you still have the number to my office?"

"I think so. Why?"

"Because I want you to call me if you need to talk."

"I'm fine."

Mark smiled at her and absently ran his knuckles down her cheek. "I know. This is just in case of anything."

She smiled ruefully. "Honestly, I'll be fine."

"Promise that you'll call if you need me."

"Mark—"

"Humor me."

She looked at him for a long moment before saying, "I promise."

Mark searched her eyes, nodding when he found the sincerity to back up her words. "Okay. I'll talk to you soon," he said, turning to leave.

Chapter Six

Mark was up before dawn the following morning, restless from a sleepless night. Ever since his wife had passed away, he had been unable to sleep for more than three hours straight. Usually, he passed the time watching old movies on television, but the events of yesterday wouldn't let him concentrate on anything other than Brooke's words of the day before.

Rising from the bed, he wearily made his way around the darkened bedroom, moving instinctively toward the door. As he walked through the hallway and into the kitchen, he couldn't help but glance out the window that provided an uninterrupted view of Brooke's house.

He noticed her house was doused in total darkness, no shadows moved beyond the open blinds. He grimaced as he noted the open invitation to criminals. Ever since he had met her, he couldn't get her to understand the importance of closing her blinds and locking her windows at night. She had continually claimed that there was no need to take those precautions. That she had lived in the house her entire life, and nothing had ever happened. Mark had the feeling that her trusting nature refused to believe that there was true evil in the world. He had the impression that she believed bad things only happened to other people. That she would never be the victim of any crime. At least that was the impression she gave until yesterday.

He briefly wondered if she slept at all last night. Her distress of the day before was genuine, and the haunted look that had been in her eyes yesterday, flashed through his mind. He hated seeing her so unsettled.

He debated as to whether or not to check on her before leaving for the office, but he quickly cast the idea aside. He didn't want to wake her if she was sleeping. He knew only too well how a good night's sleep could change someone's whole outlook on a situation.

Walking over to the coffee maker, he flicked the switch onto the 'on' position. He leaned a shoulder wearily against the wall, and absently ran a hand over his face, as he waited impatiently for the coffee to begin to brew. As he heard the rumble of the machine, he reached for a mug and thought about the conversation he had with Brooke yesterday. The information she supplied on Rick Cory was considerable, and he hoped something would show on the reports and background checks he requested on the people she mentioned. With any luck, the reports would be on his desk by the time he got to the office.

As the coffee started flowing, he removed the glass carafe and held his cup below the steady stream of liquid. He waited until the mug was nearly full before removing it and placing the coffeepot back into its space. Quickly fixing his beverage, he took a deep gulp, and casually glanced at the kitchen clock, noting the time. It was early enough that if he left for the station now, he could go over the evidence that they found yesterday, without the constant interruptions that would occur once everybody started arriving at work. The thought held a lot of appeal. Finishing his first cup of coffee, he poured another before heading toward the shower. Thirty minutes later, he was on his way to his office.

The sun was just beginning to break through the darkness as Mark walked into the police station. Traffic was light in the early morning hours, and only a few cars were on the road, allowing him to get to the office in record time. As he walked through the double glass doors, he caught a glimpse of the clock over the front desk. It wasn't even six.

He passed the desk sergeant, nodding his head in greeting as he made his way to where the automatic coffee maker rested. Pouring a cup of the thick brew, he was about to walk into his office when he noticed Megan Smith out of the corner of his eye. "Megan," he called out.

Megan turned at the sound of her name, and she

smiled when she saw Mark. Adjusting the heavy tote bag on her shoulder, she walked over to him. "Hi. You're here early," she said, lifting a travel mug to her lips and taking a sip.

"I was just thinking the same thing about you. Is everything okay? I thought you didn't start until nine."

She shrugged good-naturedly and ran a careless hand through her hair. "I wanted to get a running start on the day. With all the excitement yesterday, I'm afraid some of the other caseloads didn't get the attention they need."

"Your dedication is going to make the rest of your colleagues look bad," he teased lightly, knowing she stayed at the beach longer than the rest of her team as she oversaw the completion of the evidence collection process.

"You're one to talk," she quipped.

He smiled. "Do you know if the reports are completed on the evidence uncovered at the beach yesterday?"

"They should be on your desk. I stayed late last night to make sure you would have them first thing this morning."

"Good. I'm anxious to go over them."

"I knew you would be. Fair warning, though. The strand of hair that Walt found is dyed, and that particular shade of color is very common."

"How common?"

"It matches mine. That should give you an idea."

Mark almost laughed at the way she casually revealed that she dyed her hair. Most women would go to any length to keep that a secret, but not Megan. Her openness and honesty were two of the qualities he enjoyed most about her. "Thanks for the heads up. I'd better go and see what we're dealing with."

"All right. Shout if you need anything."

"Thanks. I'll talk to you later," he said, and walked into his office to begin his day.

Mark placed his cup on his desk before moving over to the closed window blinds. Opening the slats, he looked out, noting that traffic was still light and the parking lot was all but empty. He knew it would be only a matter of time before the station began to fill with people. Wanting a little solitude to get his thoughts in order, he walked back to his desk, his mind already shifting into gear as he thought about what he wanted to accomplish.

Thirty minutes later, he had finished reading through the reports and was in the process of writing a few notes when there was a brief knock on the glass panel of the door, followed by Walt's voice.

Walt entered the room without waiting for an invitation. "Morning," he said lifting a can of soda to his mouth.

Mark grimaced at Walt's choice of beverage. "Morning," he returned before gesturing to the brightly colored can. "How can you drink that stuff so early in the morning?"

"Very easily," Walt said as he took another deep drink, the cold liquid quenching both his thirst and his craving for sugar. "You should try it one morning instead of the coffee."

"No thanks."

Walt laughed at the obvious distaste in Mark's voice

and motioned to the manila folders on his desk. "Are those the reports on our victim?"

"Yeah."

"Anything interesting?" Walt asked as he sat down in the straight-back chair across from Mark.

Mark took a sip of his rapidly cooling coffee. "Read it for yourself."

Walt placed his can of soda on the desk and picked up the first folder. His eyes scanned the contents, his forehead creased in a frown as he read. "The bullet was from a 9-millimeter pistol," he murmured without looking up.

"Yeah. And according to the bloodstain pattern analysis, the shooting was done at close range."

Walt leaned back in his chair, his long legs stretched out before him. "It looks like the guy died instantly. There's nothing in this report to even hint that he might have died from drowning."

Mark looked at Walt, studying him over the rim of his mug. "You thought that was an option?"

Walt glanced up at him. "What? That he was thrown overboard before he was actually dead?"

"Yeah."

"It was a possibility."

Mark was silent for a moment as he considered Walt's words. "I get the distinct impression that whoever killed the guy, wanted to be sure that he was dead. I don't think the murderer would have taken the chance of throwing him overboard if there was even the remotest possibility that he was alive. It would have left too great a chance for the killer to be identified if our victim had somehow managed to survive a night in the ocean."

"I don't know. They could have just assumed that the blood from the guy's wound would automatically attract the sharks. If enough of a feeding frenzy occurred, it would have effectively taken care of any evidence."

"You have a point, but I still can't see someone taking that kind of chance. Especially if they put any thought into how this was all going to play out. They may have been hoping that the sea creatures would destroy any evidence, but I doubt if they were going to leave the man's death in fate's hands."

Walt looked back down at the report, and flipped the page. "Do you think we're dealing with a man or a woman?"

Mark didn't answer the question directly, instead he motioned to the report that Walt still held. "That details in the report are just the basics. We know the guy was shot with a 9-millimeter pistol. That's an easy enough gun for either a man or woman to use."

"True."

"So we have to approach this logically. If the murder was committed during a night sail, who would be the logical companion for the guy to have on board?"

"A woman. But that's not enough information for us to make the leap that the perpetrator was a female," Walt argued.

Mark inclined his head at Walt's comment. "Granted. But the hair you found attached to his watch is listed in the report as having been dyed. Something Megan warned me about this morning. How many men do you know dye their hair?"

"Quite a bit actually," Walt said, his mind wandering

to the population in Los Angeles and the number of teens who considered blond hair with black roots the in thing.

Mark shook his head slightly. "I'm not talking about kids, or senior citizens who are afraid to get old. I'm talking about men in their prime. The majority of them don't dye their hair, and if they did, the chances of the color of that strand being popular with men are slim to none. The forensics report doesn't note any other blood evidence other than the victim's. That means there was no struggle. That the hit was clean. Based on everything we have so far, this was a surprise execution. Somebody had to do this that the guy trusted implicitly. Somebody who he wasn't threatened by."

Walt reached for his can of soda and took a sip while he digested Mark's words. "What would be the motive?"

"That's a piece of the puzzle that still remains missing. It could be a scorned girlfriend, a bad business deal, or anything else for that matter."

"Did your neighbor shed any light on the guy's lifestyle?"

"If the murder took place on Cory's boat, Brooke doesn't think that it could have been a business associate. She's claiming that he only used his boat for relaxation purposes, and that whoever was on the boat with him would have been a trusted friend."

"That doesn't rule out any lady friends."

"No, it doesn't. And right now I'm inclined to believe that it was a close acquaintance of his that actually did him in."

"It would make sense," Walt acknowledged.

"Yeah, it would. Brooke also made another comment about him that I found extremely important."

"What's that?"

"The guy had a strong aversion to guns," Mark replied.

"And she's basing that assumption on . . ."

"She's basing it on the fact that Rick Cory's son was killed by a bullet meant for him. Or at the very least, meant to scare him."

Walt's eyes widened at the words. "Who pulled the trigger?"

"A woman by the name of Ellen Manning. Her husband, Arthur, was killed by one of Cory's clients."

"Accidentally?" Walt asked.

"So the guy claimed."

"I take it the defendant walked and the lady wanted revenge."

"You take it right."

"Did anything come in on the couple?"

"No. The woman's serving a life sentence. And there are no family members listed in the report that may have held a grudge against Rick Cory."

Walt reached for another folder. "Is this the background report on Cory?"

"Yeah. We were lucky that Brooke was able to immediately identify him."

"Yeah, we were fortunate on that score. But even if she hadn't, the label on the prescription bottle was still legible. We would have identified the victim eventually, especially since we had that as a clue."

Mark gestured to the report that Walt held.

"Unfortunately, the report doesn't state much. There's no family listed anyway, which coincides with what Brooke had told me yesterday. I had a couple of uniforms go to Cory's residence with a search warrant, but the place was clean. At least there was nothing there that's going to shed any light on this investigation."

"And the boat that came up registered to his name?" Walt asked.

"It's at the marina by the inlet. By the time the uniforms got there yesterday, it was docked. I had forensics go over it with a fine-tooth comb, but it doesn't look like they picked up much."

"No hair that matches the strand we found on the guy?" Walt asked, his mind racing as he tried to think of possibilities.

"No. Unfortunately, if it was his boat that the murder took place on, someone cleaned up after themselves extremely well. There wasn't even a trash bag left on board."

Walt nodded somewhat distractedly and closed the report, a frustrated expression on his face. "What else was your neighbor able to tell you?"

"Basically what I've already said. We just have to keep in mind that the guy was a defense attorney. There's always the chance that our killer was someone who held a grudge against him."

"Time will tell."

"That it will."

"So where do we go from here?" Walt asked.

"I'd like to check out the guy's boat personally."

"I'm game."

"I just need to clear up a few things here first," Mark said, motioning to the files on his desk.

"No problem. While you're doing that, I'll give my wife a call and check in on her."

Mark glanced at his watch. "It's kind of early, isn't it?"

"Nah. She told me last night that she was going to Cassadaga this morning. She should be up and getting ready."

"Cassadaga?"

"Yeah, it's a spiritual community she goes to a lot."

"I think I remember seeing a sign for the place on the interstate," Mark said.

Walt reached up to rub the back of his neck. "Well, they have a community center there where all they do is readings."

"Readings?"

"Yeah. You know. Psychic readings."

"Carol is into that?"

"More than I care to admit," Walt replied, his tone full of chagrin.

Mark lifted a shoulder expressively. "Hey, to each their own."

"Don't let Carol hear you say that so cavalierly. She takes this stuff very seriously. It's how we met actually."

"What do you mean?"

"I met her at a psychic fair. My niece wanted to go, and being the good uncle that I am, I agreed to take her. I met Carol while waiting outside the booth for my niece."

"You're joking."

"Nope."

Mark leaned back in his chair, rocking slightly. A smile hovered around his mouth. "Did you have your fortune told?"

A sheepish expression crossed Walt's face. "Carol asked if I would go in with her."

"And of course you did."

"Hey. I wanted her to have dinner with me that night. If she would have asked me to go swimming with her at midnight under a full moon, I wouldn't have hesitated for a moment."

"You had it that bad?"

"You don't know the half of it."

Mark laughed. "Carol's going there today, huh?"

"Yeah. She really gets a kick out of it. But, hey, I'm the one ruining our vacation. If she wants to waste the morning out there, who am I to say no? She took time off of work to go to California. And now that we're not going, she should be able to spend her days any way she wants."

"I can't argue with that," Mark admitted before asking, "It doesn't bother you that she spends money on this type of thing?"

"It makes her happy."

"Does it make you happy?"

Walt smiled. "If Carol's happy, then I'm happy."

"Ah."

"What does that mean?"

"Nothing."

"Don't give me that. That one 'ah' meant something."

Mark laughed. "You're imagining things."

"I don't think so."

Mark shook his head slightly, a slight smile playing around his mouth. "Go make your call while I make some headway with this mess," he said, gesturing to the items on his desk.

"Not a problem," Walt said as he walked to the door. "Let me know when you're ready to go."

"I will."

Chapter Seven

Later that morning, Mark drove to the marina. The place was crawling with people, many of whom were getting ready to take their boats out for a late morning sail. The strength of the sun was just beginning to make itself known, and people seemed to be heading out to enjoy the water before the impending afternoon rain.

Mark glanced at the clock on the dashboard. "I was hoping that we would avoid the crowds."

Walt shrugged nonchalantly as he watched the people prepare their boats. "It's summertime and the kids are out of school."

"I know."

"You had to expect that people would gravitate toward the water," Walt said matter-of-factly.

"I didn't expect it this early. I thought we still had time to beat the rush. I just hope that nobody went on the guy's boat. I had some uniforms tape it off, but that could have proved more of an open invitation than anything else."

"We could always have it pulled from the water and taken in for forensic testing. Maybe there's something that the technicians missed."

"Yeah, I thought about it. But I'm curious to see if the perpetrator will come back to the boat."

"If the crime was even committed on the guy's sailboat."

"I'm leaning toward the fact that it was. At least that would make sense," Mark said.

"True. But it would also mean that the murderer would have to have a working knowledge of how to sail. The report from this morning didn't find any marks on the outside of the vessel. Somebody would have had to know exactly how to dock the boat without damaging it."

"I know. But that won't prevent the killer from retracing their steps if they're the nervous type. It's possible that whoever did this may come back to make sure that they didn't leave anything behind."

Walt grunted. "Coming back would be a pretty careless act on their part. Up until now, nothing we have would suggest that type of move. It wouldn't fit the profile of such a clean killing."

"No killing is ever clean. You just have to know where to find the evidence," Mark said.

"Well, if the perpetrator did come back to the boat, it could prove messy for them. They would definitely be taking a risk that their identity would be discovered."

"People do strange things when they're under stress.

You never know what to expect. Guilt has a way of eating people up inside."

"I don't know if we have to worry about the person feeling guilty. Based on the lack of evidence we have to go on right now, I would say that we're dealing with someone who doesn't have a conscience. Someone who had this planned down to the last detail."

Mark looked over at him knowingly. "You believe the killer is a cold-blooded individual."

"Don't you?"

Mark shrugged. "Cold-blooded or just able to cover their tracks well."

Walt reached up to adjust the bill of his baseball cap. "They covered up their actions too well."

"What do you mean?"

Walt hesitated for a moment. "Let me ask you something."

"Sure."

"Just how well do you know your neighbor?"

"Brooke?"

"Yeah. I mean, you haven't even been in town a year."

"So?"

"So, how well do you truly know her?"

"Well enough."

"You don't think it's possible that Brooke is somehow involved in this mess?" Walt asked carefully, unsure of how his question would be perceived. He had been thinking of a way to broach the subject ever since he had walked out of Mark's office earlier that morning. The woman was a wealth of information on Rick Cory, and there was the fact that she had a past with the victim, a broken engagement that may have left hard feelings on her part.

Mark stared at Walt in stunned disbelief before giving a bark of laughter. "You have to be joking."

Walt glanced at him, his expression serious. "I'm not."

"You've met Brooke. You had to have realized by now that she just doesn't have the temperament to have done what you're suggesting."

"Everybody's capable of murder given the right set of circumstances. You've been around long enough to know that."

"But Brooke? The lady couldn't hurt a fly."

Walt sighed. "Look, I'm not suggesting that she was involved, but I don't think it would hurt to run a background check on her. The woman did break her engagement with the guy. Maybe there's something in her past that we should be aware of."

"Come on, Walt. People break off engagements all the time. That doesn't mean that they're involved in crimes."

"True. But that doesn't mean they're not capable of wanting some sort of revenge," Walt shot back.

"But murder?"

"It's not out of the realm of possibilities."

"No," Mark admitted. "It's not. But Brooke's not like that."

"I never said she was. I'm just saying that maybe it wouldn't hurt to check her out. To see if there's something in her past."

"She told me that she had no hard feelings toward the guy."

"She probably doesn't. But there's also the chance that there's more history here than she's letting on."

"I doubt it. She would have told me."

"Why? Because of what she already told you? What if she's trying to hide something?"

"She has nothing to hide," Mark shot back, beginning to get aggravated with Walt's words.

"Hey, calm down. I'm not accusing her of anything. I just think that we should cover all of our bases."

"What you're saying doesn't make sense."

"Maybe it doesn't make sense because you're too close to the situation."

"And maybe you're just grasping at straws."

"Maybe," Walt conceded, deciding that he should back off a little on the subject of Brooke.

Mark took a deep breath and sighed. Running a hand around the back of his neck, he began to knead the muscles that were beginning to get tight. "Look, I didn't mean to jump on you."

"I know."

"But my gut is telling me that Brooke wasn't directly involved."

"Hey. We'll drop the subject. No sweat. Like you said, I'm probably just grasping at straws. I hate not having any answers."

Mark stared at Walt for a moment before saying, "Yeah, me too."

Walt inclined his head in acknowledgement of the words. "Then let's go and check out this guy's boat. Maybe we'll luck out and find something."

"That's what I'm hoping for." Mark led the way to the dock. He had to dodge a little kid on a bicycle that came barreling toward him. "Whoa," he muttered as the kid laughed gleefully.

Walt laughed. "If he keeps going at that rate, he's going to run straight off the end of the dock."

"I wonder where his parents are," Mark said as he glanced around the area. Though the dock was crowded, everybody was mulling around doing their own thing, not paying attention to much else going on around them.

"I'm sure they're around somewhere," Walt said, stepping onto the floating dock. "Man, I hate these things," he muttered as the wooden slats swayed gently under his weight.

"I thought you would be accustomed to them being from California."

"Why do you say that?"

Mark shrugged. "You always gave me the impression that you were a beach person."

"I am. But the key word is beach. As in sand. Solid ground. I've never been on a boat in my life."

"Never?"

"Not once."

"That's hard to believe."

"It's true."

"Then this will be a new experience for you," Mark said as they walked along the dock.

"I'm always up for a new experience. Just where is his dock slip anyway?"

Mark looked at the docked boats. "It should be right around here. The name of the boat is *Cory's Pleasure.*"

Walt grunted. "I never understood where people came up with the names for their boats."

"I know what you mean," Mark said just as he spotted the yellow police tape around a gleaming white sailboat. "There it is."

Walt followed his gaze. "It doesn't look like the tape was disturbed at all."

Walt waited until Mark stepped on board the boat before crouching down to slide between the tape. He held onto the side of the boat as it rocked. "Man, I hate this."

Mark laughed, while he glanced around with interest. He noted the gleaming chrome, and the sparkling white fiberglass of the vessel. "The uniforms weren't kidding when they said this place was spotless. If the guy was actually killed on this boat, somebody did a great job of cleaning up."

"Too good of a job."

Mark walked over to the side seating and absently ran a finger against the cushion. "It's wet."

Walt looked over at him. "What?"

"The cushion. It's wet."

"So?"

"So, it shouldn't be."

Walt glanced around. "Maybe the boat next to it splashed when it was coming in," he said, trying to offer an explanation.

"Maybe. Or maybe someone's been on board." Mark crouched down and looked through the windows of the cabin.

"Do you see anything?"

"I'm not sure."

"What do you mean, you're not sure?"

"Just that," Mark said as he motioned for Walt to be quiet. Reaching for his gun, he pulled it from his shoulder harness.

Walt's eyebrows drew together in a frown, and he automatically reached for his own gun.

Mark got up from his crouched position and carefully eased his way around the boat to the front hull. Motioning to Walt to cover the back entrance, he lifted the small hatch door that led to the cabin. He looked up and caught Walt's eye. Knowing that he was being covered, he carefully eased himself through the opening, landing on the floor with barely a sound.

The cabin was dark, only a partial bit of sunlight seeped through the small windows. Mark's eyes caught a shadow, and he carefully made his way over to it, his steps light and soundless. His gun cocked, he held it trained on his target. "Police! Freeze!"

The person in the cabin froze at the sound of his voice.

"Turn around slowly," Mark said, feeling a rush as the adrenaline pumped through his body.

The shadowy figure turned, and Mark stared for a moment in stunned disbelief. It was Brooke Jennings.

Chapter Eight

"Brooke!"

"Mark," she said softly, not believing that he had found her in such a compromising position. She briefly closed her eyes, trying to think of the best way to explain what she was doing on board the boat, but every thought that flashed through her mind sounded lame, even to herself. Mark took his job seriously. She doubted he was going to appreciate any explanation she could offer.

"What are you doing here?" he demanded, his mind flashing back to Walt's comments a little earlier. Was it possible that she was somehow involved in the murder? His mind refused to accept the idea, but her presence on the boat seemed to suggest otherwise.

"I can explain."

"I'm listening."

Brooke took a deep breath, her eyes falling to the

gun in his hand. She motioned to the weapon. "Could you put that away?"

Mark looked down at his gun. The weapon was a natural part of his life, and he was entirely comfortable with it in his grasp. He forgot that another person might not have the same view of the fact that it was just an extension of who he was. He glanced back at her, noticing the slight tensing of her body as she stared at the gun, and he couldn't help but wonder if she actually believed he might use it on her. "Does it make you nervous?"

"Shouldn't it?"

Mark shrugged and jammed the gun back into his holster. "No. Not as long as it's me who's holding it."

"I haven't had much experience with guns. I'd like to keep it that way."

"Then you shouldn't go trespassing where you have no business being," he replied more harshly than he intended, unable to suppress his disappointment and anger at finding her on board the boat.

"I told you that I can explain."

"And I told you that I'm listening. So go ahead."

Brooke glanced around the darkened cabin. "Can we go above deck?"

Mark's eyes narrowed slightly. "Why?"

"I feel closed in down here," she admitted, beginning to feel lightheaded from the lack of air circulating. The Florida sun beat mercilessly down on the boat, and the tinted windows of the cabin did little to keep the interior cool. The combination of the humidity and heat was stifling in the enclosed space.

"Then you shouldn't be down here in the first place."

"Mark—"

"No, Brooke. I think we'll stay right where we are while you explain why you're here."

"But . . ." she began just as Walt Tyler came down the ladder.

"Mark," Walt called, his eyes trying to adjust to the dimness of the cabin.

"Over here, Walt."

Walt turned. His eyes widened as he caught sight of the person standing beside Mark, and his hand automatically tightened on his gun. "Is everything all right?"

Mark sighed. "Yeah."

Walt nodded and walked closer to where the two people stood. The person with Mark stood with their back to him, and he couldn't make out their features. "What's going on?"

Mark looked at Brooke. "You remember Walt, don't you?"

Brooke nodded slightly and turned to acknowledge Walt. "It's nice to see you again," she said, unsure of what the proper etiquette was in a situation like this.

Walt's eyes widened at the identity of the visitor and his eyes shot up to make contact with Mark's. "What's she doing here?"

Mark lifted a shoulder expressively. "She was just getting ready to explain it. You don't mind going back up on deck to make sure that we don't get anymore unwanted visitors, do you?"

Walt stared at him a moment longer. "Are you sure?" he asked, glancing back at Brooke with obvious mistrust.

Mark wanted to laugh, except the situation was far from funny. Whether Brooke knew it or not, by coming on board this boat, she had automatically made herself a suspect. "Yeah, I'm sure."

Walt paused a moment longer, not wanting to leave them alone. "All right, I'll go back up on deck. But give a shout if you need me."

"I will." Mark watched while Walt carefully made his way back up on deck. As soon as he cleared the small room, Mark turned back to Brooke. "Okay, explain."

Brooke looked up at his face, noting the sternness of his features. If she didn't know Mark personally, she would have been back up on deck with Walt. It just occurred to her how intimidating he could be. She was surprised that she hadn't noticed it before. She supposed it was because he had never been anything but kind to her, but looking at him now, she couldn't help but think that she was getting her first glimpse of his chief of police persona.

"Brooke?" Mark prompted as she just stood there, staring at him silently.

Brooke took a deep breath. "You want to know why I'm here," she hedged, still trying to think of the best way to explain the situation.

Mark sighed at her obvious stall tactic. "You know that I do."

She nodded, staring at him in silence while she gathered her thoughts.

"Brooke? I'm waiting."

Brooke paused a moment longer before she responded. "I wanted to see if I could find anything that would help solve Rick's murder."

"You didn't trust me to do my job?"

"That's not it at all." She began to move restlessly about the small space, trying to work off some of her nervous energy. The floor creaked slightly as she walked, and she cringed inwardly at how foolish she was to have come on board by herself. If it was anyone but Mark who found her, she would have effectively trapped herself within the confines of the cabin. The creaking of the floor would have been a dead giveaway if she had tried to leave.

Mark studied her in the dim light. Even in the shadows of the cabin, he could see the paleness of her features. "Talk to me, Brooke. Tell me what you hoped to find," he said while he watched every nuance of her facial expression, of her mannerisms, hoping to see something, anything that would alleviate the suspicious feeling he suddenly felt toward her and her possible involvement with the murder.

"Yesterday, after you left, I couldn't shake the feeling that there was something I should have told you. Something that might help with the investigation of Rick's death."

"What was it?"

"When I was dating Rick, we used to go sailing a lot. We used to plan our future while we were on the water. And during one of those sails, Rick showed me a compartment he had built into the boat to store valuables. It was waterproof in case the boat ever took on water."

Mark's thoughts went back to the report he had on his desk regarding the boat. There was no such notation in the data. "Why didn't you call me on the phone when you remembered?"

"It didn't occur to me," she replied honestly. "I only recalled it this morning, and then the only thought that was on my mind was to check it out. I wanted to see if there was anything stored in the compartment that might be useful in finding Rick's killer."

"You should have called me the moment you remembered," he insisted, not trusting her explanation or its plausibility.

Brooke sighed, hearing the obvious distrust in his voice. "I know, but I wasn't thinking clearly."

At her words, Mark realized that she wasn't going to expand on her explanation. He didn't know if the reason was because she was telling him the truth, or if it was because there was something she was trying to hide. He took a deep breath, and tried to make sense of her presence on the boat. "You shouldn't be here," he felt compelled to say.

She inclined her head in acknowledgement. "I realize that it wasn't the smartest move, but at one time, Rick was the closest person to me."

"That doesn't justify your presence here."

"I know, but please try and understand. My relationship with Rick lasted for two years. I can't just pretend that it didn't exist. I can't just sit back and not do anything to help find his murderer."

"You're not sitting back and doing nothing. The information you gave me yesterday was a big help."

"But there's more that I can be doing."

"Like what? Searching a place that you have no business being at? You have to realize that you can't stay here. It was reckless even coming here today. Don't you realize what could have happened?"

"I was careful."

"Right," he scoffed. "You were so careful that I found you."

Brooke wanted to argue with him over his choice of words, but she couldn't. She had been thinking the same thing just a few minutes ago. "You have to understand why I came."

"I hate to tell you this, but I don't understand. I know you had a close relationship with Rick at one time. But that doesn't rationalize putting your life at risk by coming here."

"It does if I can find anything that would help solve Rick's murder," she replied adamantly.

Mark sighed at her words. "Brooke—"

"Please."

Mark realized that she wasn't going to let this rest until she found what she was looking for. Every professional instinct he had wanted to stop her. He knew she was ruining the integrity of the evidence with her presence, but he couldn't bring himself to call a halt to her search just yet. He was curious if she would be able to find something. Something that his own technicians may have missed. Glancing around, he looked for the light switch. "It would probably be a little easier to find whatever it is that you're looking for if you had some light," he said, his words expressing his reluctant willingness to let her search the room.

Brooke shot him a grateful smile and immediately walked over to the control panel to flick a switch. Instantly the cabin was flooded with light. "I didn't want to draw any attention to myself," she explained, noting his raised eyebrows at her familiarity with the cabin.

"Uh huh."

She held up three fingers. "Scout's honor."

"Mm. So tell me, where exactly is this compartment?"

"It should be somewhere over here," she said, walking over to the teak paneling on the wall. She knocked lightly with her knuckles, listening to the deep vibrations of the echoes as she hit both hollow and solid spots.

Mark watched her closely, noting her unfamiliarity with the exact location of where the compartment was located. "I thought you said he showed it to you."

"He did. I just have to find the release." She ran her fingers along the edge of the wood's groove, searching for the pressure point that would open the panel.

"Brooke . . ." he warned when she couldn't locate the catch. He began to wonder if one even existed. He began to wonder if she was being truthful regarding her reason for being on the boat.

Brooke was oblivious to his thoughts. She continued to search the wall. "I know it's here somewhere," she said just as she hit the point that caused the panel to be released.

Mark's eyebrows rose as the compartment opened, and he immediately stepped forward as his eyes caught a flash of color against the interior edge of the opening. "Don't touch anything," he warned.

"Why?"

"Because it looks like there might be blood inside."

Chapter Nine

"Blood!" she repeated.

"Step back," Mark said, reaching for her arm and gently pulling her behind him. He looked over at the stream of sunlight that filtered into the cabin from the opening that led up on deck. "Walt!" he shouted before turning back to the space that Brooke had just revealed. He wondered how his own people could have missed this in the initial search. They were usually methodical about searching an area. Though the police department in town was small by big city standards, the quality of personnel were on the same level as any big city precinct.

Walt came rushing down the ladder. "What's the matter?"

Mark gestured to the space that was just revealed. "Take a look."

Walt frowned and walked over to the teak paneling.

Seeing the open compartment, he turned to Mark. "Who found this?"

"Brooke."

Walt turned to look at Brooke. "Is this what you came on board the boat to find?"

"Yes. I only remembered this morning that Rick had the compartment built into the wall."

Walt looked back to the opening. "That looks like a blood streak inside."

"I know," Mark acknowledged, turning to face Brooke. "Did Rick ever mention what he wanted to store in the compartment? Why he had it built?"

"No, at least nothing specific. He just wanted a safe place to store things in case he needed it. He spent a lot of time on his boat." She motioned to the stain. "Do you think it's Rick's blood?"

"I don't know. We'll know more after we have it tested," Mark said as he reached inside his pocket for a pair of latex gloves. Quickly donning them, he walked closer to the panel door and reached for it, examining the sides.

"I'm going to go up on deck and call the station to get a search team out here," Walt said as he walked over to the ladder and quickly made his way up on deck.

Brooke looked around the cabin once more. "Maybe there's something else here," she said softly, almost as if she was talking to herself.

"Maybe. But you're not going to stay here and look for it," Mark said, not even bothering to glance in her direction. His full attention was on the evidence they had just uncovered.

"Why not?"

"Because you have no business being here."

"But, Mark . . ."

Mark turned to look at her. "You do realize that you broke the law in coming here, don't you?"

"Broke the law? I didn't do anything."

"How about trespassing?"

"But I explained why I was here."

"Yes, you did. But that doesn't negate the fact that you're here when you have absolutely no business being here. Don't you realize that your presence on this boat casts suspicion on you?"

Brooke stared at him in stunned disbelief. "You don't honestly believe that I had anything to do with the murder."

When Mark stared at her silently without commenting, Brooke continued, "That's ridiculous."

"Is it?"

"Of course it is!" she said, hurt that he would actually think such a thing. She thought they were friends. She wasn't prepared for the amount of betrayal she felt at his casually spoken words. She looked into his eyes and saw the question in them, and she could almost see the doubts running through his mind. "Come on, Mark. Be realistic. I could never do what you're suggesting. I thought you knew me by now."

Mark sensed the undercurrent of emotion in her voice, and he knew instinctively that she was hurt by his words, by their meaning. The thought bothered him. He honestly liked Brooke, and he was having a hard time connecting her to the crime. But by her own admission, Brooke did have a strong past with the victim. His common sense began warring with his heart. He knew realistically that he should take her into the station. Regardless of whether or not she had anything to do with the killing, she had definitely broken the law the moment she stepped onto the boat. Not only had she violated a police crime scene, but she had effectively contaminated any additional evidence present. Whether Brooke wanted to admit it or not, she had royally screwed up. Evidence from her own person was now on the boat, and forensics wasn't sophisticated enough to determine the exact time of everything. But as he noticed the hurt in her eyes, he couldn't bring himself to take her down to the station. He rationalized that she lived right next door to him. That he could pick her up at any time if she stepped out of line again, or if they made a strong enough connection between her and the case to validate an arrest. A possibility that seemed to be getting stronger with every passing moment.

"Brooke—"

"Tell me that you don't think I had anything to do with this," she demanded, her eyes holding his, daring him to say it aloud.

Mark stared at her in silence.

"Mark . . ."

Her concern regarding his opinion was clear in her voice, and he found he couldn't deny her the words she wanted to hear. He paused for only a second. "I don't believe that you had anything to do with this," he told her, more as pacification than anything else.

Brooke studied him silently for a moment, trying to read the sincerity of his expression, of his body language. Finding nothing that would outwardly shout that he wasn't being truthful, she inclined her head slightly. "Thank you."

"I still need you to go home."

"Home?"

"Yes. As I said, you don't belong here. I'm not going to jeopardize my job or Walt's by allowing you to stay."

"I wouldn't expect you to," she said, startled by his words. She hadn't thought of her presence on the boat in quite that light, but thinking about it now, his words made sense.

Mark watched her thoughtfully. "No more amateur sleuthing."

"No more."

"Okay. Then let's see if we can get you out of here without any problems."

Brooke nodded. "Mark?"

"Yes?"

"For what it's worth, I'm sorry."

"For what it's worth, so am I." He escorted her back on deck to where Walt stood.

Walt had just flipped his cell phone closed when they stepped on deck. His eyes met Mark's. "They'll be here shortly."

Mark inclined his head. "Good. Brooke's going home. Can you escort her to her car?"

Brooke glanced at Mark sharply. "That's not necessary."

"I think it is," Mark replied, his dark sunglasses now in place, hiding the expression in his eyes.

"I can get to my car myself."

"Probably, but I'm not willing to take the chance that somebody's watching the place."

"Nobody's watching the place. If they were, one of us would have noticed it," she replied.

"Possibly. But unless you can prove it unequivocally, Walt will see you to your car."

Brooke wanted to argue with him, but one look at his set features had her biting back the words. Now wasn't the time to get into it with him. There were too many people around. Too much of a chance of the wrong words being said. "Fine."

Mark glanced over at Walt. "Make sure she gets in the car okay, and then check out the area. I'll wait here."

"No problem," Walt said as he turned and escorted Brooke, holding a hand out to her as she made the leap onto the dock.

"Brooke," Mark said, his voice carrying above the numerous voices from the other boats.

She turned. "Yes?"

"I'll talk to you soon," Mark said.

"Soon," she repeated before turning and walking with Walt to her car.

Mark waited until they were out of sight before he walked back over to the companionway and went below deck. He took off his sunglasses to let his eyes again adjust to the dimness of the cabin, and he carefully walked around the area, searching for additional evidence.

A hint of metal caught his eye and he looked down at the carpet, noticing a small gold hoop earring. An image of Brooke sitting on the sofa yesterday flashed through his mind, and he knew exactly where he had seen the earring before. It had been on her earlobe. She had her ears double pierced, and almost always just wore a simple pair of diamond studs. But yesterday, one of her ears had sported a hoop. At the time, he hadn't thought much over the fact that she was wearing only one gold earring. As far as he knew, it was some new type of fashion statement. But finding this earring now, cast a different light on the picture.

He picked up the earring before carefully placing it in a small plastic bag. He studied the object, noting that it was probably a common piece of jewelry, easily obtained from any department store or kiosk in the mall. He also had to consider the fact that Brooke was just on the boat, that she could have lost it today. But somehow, he couldn't bring himself to believe that. He wished he could come right out and ask her about the earring, but he knew he couldn't. She was too sensitive, too intelligent. Considering the fact that he had never once in the entire time he had known her questioned her jewelry, she would have to know that he was asking for a reason.

He ran a hand across his eyes and down his face, as he thought of the implication. No matter how hard he tried, he couldn't seem to let go of the fact that Brooke may somehow be involved in this mess. The thought was not comforting.

The sound of footsteps had him turning toward the hatch.

Walt lowered himself into the tightly confined space. "Hey."

"Did Brooke get off okay?"

"Yeah, no problems."

Mark sighed. "I didn't expect to find her here."

Walt's eyebrows lifted. "Yeah, that kind of threw me for a loop too," he said, noticing that Mark was holding something. He motioned to the object. "What's that?"

Mark held up the bag, revealing the potential piece of evidence. "I found an earring."

"Just now?"

"Yeah. Brooke has a pair exactly like it."

Walt reached for the bag and studied the earring. "Are you sure?"

"Almost positive. I'll see if I can confirm it."

"How? You can't come right out and ask."

"No, but I'll think of something."

Walt handed the small bag back. "It was kind of strange that she knew about that compartment, wasn't it?"

"A little. But she was seeing the guy for two years."

"Do you think there's a chance that something other than blood will show up in the evidence that we just discovered?"

"I don't know. With any luck, we'll find something else that we can tie into this case. At the very least, we'll know if the blood belongs to our victim."

"Mm," Walt said before casually adding, "You know, I've been thinking. Brooke's hair could be a match to the one we found snagged on the victim's watch."

Mark looked at him, his eyes slightly narrowed. "So could Carol's, or any other number of women. Even

Megan mentioned that the color was an exact match to her own."

"Brooke's the only one that's claiming any association to the victim," Walt reminded him.

"If Brooke was really involved in this, what would she have to gain by trying to help with the investigation? She's not stupid. She would have to realize that it would cast a shadow of doubt on her."

Walt shrugged. "Who knows how the mind works. Maybe she's in denial. Maybe we're dealing with a split personality."

"Split personality, huh?" Mark repeated, practically scoffing.

"It's possible."

"Anything's possible," Mark agreed, his mind processing what Walt had said, but quickly discarding it. He had dealt too long with people to believe in the concept. He had even been on a case where the killer had walked free after claiming insanity, claiming multiple personalities. The guy's lawyer had somehow gotten a psychiatrist to validate the prognosis. The ruse had worked in the courtroom and with the jury, but sixty days after being released from the mental hospital with a clean bill of health, the punk had killed again.

"Could I ask you something?" Walt asked, not looking at Mark as he walked around the cabin.

"Sure."

"Why didn't you arrest Brooke?"

"For being here today?"

"Yeah. She broke the law."

Mark sighed and ran a hand over the back of his neck. "I know."

"So?"

"So, I decided that she's not a threat," Mark told him, not wanting to say that he let her go because he lived next door to her and could keep an eye on her. He didn't like the fact that Walt was focusing on her involvement, almost pushing her into the number one suspect slot.

"Based on?"

"Based on the fact that it's my decision."

"Ah."

"What does that mean?"

"Nothing. It was just an expression."

Mark looked over at him, his eyes pure steel. "Don't worry about Brooke. I'll take care of her."

"I'm sure you will."

"Walt," Mark warned.

"Hey, I didn't mean anything by it. I'm just trying to cover all the angles."

"I don't want you harassing her."

Walt managed to look offended. "I would never do that."

"Your record suggests otherwise."

"Hey, relax. I'm no fool. I have no desire to tangle with you," Walt promised, wondering about the amount of protectiveness Mark seemed to have for Brooke Jennings. It was the first time he noticed that Mark wasn't going to play this strictly by the rules. The concept threw him for a moment. Mark had never seen things in shades of gray. Everything was always black or white. There was no meeting in the middle. Right was right, wrong was wrong. The fact that he was making concessions now was totally out of character.

Mark studied him for a moment. "Good. Because I have no desire to go to war with you either," he told him, with the underlying message that he would, should the need arise.

Walt's eyes widened slightly at Mark's words. He knew Mark could be ruthless when crossed. He had seen him in action. He had no desire to find out just how ruthless he could be firsthand. "Like I said, this is your call."

"As long as we understand each other."

"We do," Walt assured him. "I promise I'll keep Brooke's name out of our future conversations."

"I don't care if you mention Brooke. I just don't want her to be the main focus of this case. At least not until we have some concrete evidence to support the idea."

"Then you're not totally convinced that she's not involved?" Walt asked, somewhat relieved that Mark was still open to all possibilities.

"Let's just say that I want to see what materializes."

"Fair enough," Walt said before holding out a hand. "Hand me a pair of your gloves, will you? Let's see if we can find anything else in this shoebox while we wait for our team to arrive."

Mark studied him for a moment longer before reaching inside his pocket. "Sure," he said, handing him the items requested.

"Any preference on where to start?" Walt asked as he donned the gloves.

"No. I want to take the place apart. The investigators that were here yesterday were sloppy in the search. I don't want to take any chances that there's something else here that they may have missed."

"Amen to that."

"So, let's get started."

Chapter Ten

In the darkness of the early morning hours, Mark once again gave up trying to sleep. Turning restlessly on the bed, he glanced at his bedside clock. It wasn't even four o'clock. With a sigh of resignation, he thought about the long morning in front of him. His days seemed endless lately, and he wished that he could get back into a regular sleep cycle. It would at least put some sense of normality into his life. Deciding that he needed to get out of bed before he went totally stir crazy, he rose and walked barefoot through the quiet house to the kitchen, stopping only long enough to turn on the television.

After starting the automatic coffee maker, he went back into the living room and sat on the sofa. Reaching for the remote control, he scanned past the infomercials, searching for something to watch. Anything to pass some time. Settling on an old western, he put his feet up on the coffee table and waited impatiently for the coffee to brew.

Minutes later, he heard the rumbling of the machine that indicated the coffee was done. Adjusting the volume on the television set so that he could hear it from the other room, he went back into the kitchen.

He poured a mug of the strong coffee and reached for the sugar, his eyes automatically looking out the window to Brooke's house. His forehead creased in a frown when he noticed that her lights were on. The house shone like a beacon in the darkness, all of the rooms visible from his vantage point illuminated, the security lights flooding the grounds. Concern gripped him. He knew the lights weren't on a few minutes ago, and he could think of only one explanation for them to be on now. Something had to be wrong. Pausing only long enough to grab his gun, he wasted no time in heading out the door.

Mark ran to Brooke's house, vaulting over the hedges that separated their property. Once he arrived at her front porch, he pressed her doorbell. He listened intently for any sound from within, but all he heard was the chirping sound of insects from the outside grounds.

Getting impatient, Mark banged his fist on her door. "Brooke!"

The door opened suddenly, and Brooke stood in the entrance, staring at him with wide eyes. She grasped the front edges of her robe together. "Mark. What's the matter? Is something wrong?" she asked as she peered out behind him into the darkness, searching for what had gotten him so worked up. Her dog, Jake, stood protectively at her side.

"That's what I came to ask you."

"Me?"

"Yes. Are you all right?"

"Why wouldn't I be?"

Mark lifted one shoulder and sighed. "I don't know. The fact that every light in your house is on worried me."

"Every light?" she repeated, turning and glancing around as if to verify his statement.

Mark's eyes narrowed. "Are you okay?" he asked, his eyes searching her face, her figure, ensuring himself that she was all right.

Brooke ran a restless hand through her hair, touched by his obvious concern. "Yeah. I'm sorry I worried you."

"There's no need to apologize."

"I hadn't realized that I had turned on all of the lights," she said, her voice trailing off. She looked at the gun that he had gripped in his hand. "You came prepared."

"I came prepared," he returned, following her gaze. Since he had not bothered to take his holster, he had no choice but to hold the weapon as he stood there. "What happened?"

"Nothing."

"Then why is every light on?"

"I honestly don't know. I guess I just got spooked."

"Why?"

"I thought I heard something, and I got up to investigate. I hadn't realized that I was turning on the lights as I went."

Mark studied her, trying to determine if what she was saying was true. "Do you want me to check out the house?"

She smiled slightly and shook her head. "It's not

necessary," she said, feeling suddenly foolish, realizing that she probably just heard the house settling.

"I'd like to check around anyway," Mark told her, knowing that he wouldn't be able to relax until he did. "Would you mind?"

"It's really not necessary."

"Humor me."

"Mark . . ."

"Brooke . . ." he mimicked, not budging an inch.

Brooke stared at him silently, knowing that they were virtually at an impasse. She got the distinct impression that he was going nowhere until he checked out her house for himself. "If it would make you feel better," she said as she stepped back and allowed him to enter her home. She grabbed Jake's collar to prevent him from running out into the yard.

"It would," Mark replied as he stepped over the threshold, listening intently for any sounds from within. "Where did you hear the noise coming from?" he asked, when all he could detect was silence.

"I'm not sure. I just heard something," she said, releasing Jake the moment the door closed. She shook her head and looked up at him wryly. "This is silly, really. There's no need for you to waste your time. The noise I heard was probably just the house settling."

"It won't hurt for me to check things out. Why don't you stay here. This won't take long," he assured her as he began to move through the house.

Brooke ignored his instructions and followed close behind him. She saw the slight smile of reassurance that he flashed her when she gripped his arm. She would never admit it to him, but she was glad that he was here.

She had gone through the house on her own, and was satisfied that she was alone, but the events of the past couple of days had really thrown her. Her nerves were on edge and her imagination was in overdrive. His presence in the house was a welcome intervention.

Mark went through each of the rooms, checking all the closets, anywhere someone would be able to hide. "What did the noise sound like?"

"I don't know if I can describe it."

"Try."

"I guess it sounded like footsteps in the living room. Obviously, nobody's there. Like I said, it must have been the house settling."

"Probably, but I'll finish checking just in case," he told her, continuing to search the rooms.

Brooke followed right behind him, relieved by his words. "I was hoping that you would say that."

Under any other circumstances, Mark would have smiled at her words. But now wasn't the time. He couldn't forget that a man had been killed in the area. A man that had a close tie to Brooke. It took him only a few minutes to complete the search. "There's no one here," he said after he finished checking out her bedroom. They both stood in front of her dresser, and his eyes automatically noted that she was a restless sleeper. The comforter and sheets were strewn all over the floor. "Rough night?"

Brooke smiled slightly in embarrassment and quickly went to pick up the bedclothes. "No rougher than usual. Sorry about the mess."

"There's nothing to apologize for."

Her eyes met his. "That's not entirely true. About

what happened on Rick's boat. . . ." she began, her voice trailing off as she tried to think of the right words to say. She wanted to fully clear the air with him. She didn't want there to be any hard feelings between them. She had been in the wrong, regardless of her reasons behind her actions. She wanted Mark to understand that she realized that.

Mark watched her struggle to put the words together, and he felt a surge of empathy. He really didn't want to get into further discussion about the incident with her until he had some concrete evidence that there was more to her visit to the boat than she let on. "Why don't we put it down to a bad judgment call. Just promise me that you won't do anything like that again."

She held his gaze for a moment longer. "I won't." She straightened her comforter and adjusted the pillows. "I really do appreciate you coming over here, though."

"What are neighbors for," he replied as he watched her. He turned to look at her dresser, noticing the single gold hoop earring that rested in a small porcelain trinket dish. He absently reached out to pick it up. "Just one earring?" he asked, his eyes studying the earring, recognizing it as the twin to the one he found on the boat.

"What?" Brooke asked in confusion as she walked over to where he stood.

Mark held up the earring. "You just have one."

Brooke shrugged and smiled, her fingers reaching up to tug at her earlobe. "I lost one."

"When?"

"I'm not sure. I was hoping that I would find it laying around somewhere in the house."

"You don't have any idea of where you lost it?"

"Unfortunately, no. It's not the first time that particular earring has fallen out. There's something wrong with the catch. I've been meaning to take it to the jeweler to get it fixed, but I wasn't sure if it would be worth the money. They weren't very expensive."

Mark placed the earring back into the trinket dish. "I take it that they don't have sentimental value?"

"Hardly."

"Even so, it would be a shame if you couldn't find it."

"I know."

Mark glanced around the room one final time. "Well, since everything seems to be okay here, I guess I should be going."

"Don't," she said, the word out of her mouth before she could stop it.

Mark looked at her. "What?"

"Don't go. I don't want to be alone."

Mark was taken aback by her words, but was careful to keep it from showing. He knew she wasn't making the request lightly. She wasn't the type to ask for support needlessly. She pretty much depended on herself. He knew without being told that she was more unsettled than she cared to admit. "All right. I'll stay," he said, unable to leave her when she so obviously didn't want to be alone.

At his words, Brooke let out the breath that she hadn't realized she was holding, and motioned to the door. "Why don't we go and sit outside by the pool. I'll put some coffee on."

"Okay," he said, turning to lead the way. He was curious about her request for him to stay, but he didn't want to probe too deeply. He figured she would tell him if she felt the need.

As they walked through the house, Brooke stopped by the thermostat and adjusted the temperature of the air conditioner. "Let me get Jake his breakfast, and then I'll put the coffee on."

"I'll feed Jake," Mark offered, moving over to the pantry to where she kept the dog food. "It's still in the bin?" he asked as he opened the double doors.

"Yes. He gets two scoops."

"I remember," Mark said as he measured out the food. Bending down, he placed the dish on the floor and lifted the large water bowl. Moving over to the sink, he waited while Brooke filled the coffee carafe with water. The moment she stepped away, he rinsed and filled the bowl.

Brooke was watching his actions out of the corner of her eye. "You're pretty good at that."

"Pretty good at what?"

"Taking care of an animal."

Mark laughed. "It's not rocket science."

"No. But a lot of people don't like animals."

Mark bent down and fondled the dog's ears. "Well, I'm not one of them."

"I can tell."

With a final pat to the dog's silky coat, Mark stood and moved over to the counter. Leaning his back against the edge, he studied Brooke as she measured coffee into the filter. "Do you feel any better?"

She smiled slightly, but didn't look up from her task. "Much."

"I'm glad."

Brooke closed the lid on the canister that held the coffee and turned to face him. "Did anybody ever tell you what a nice man you are?"

"Does my mother count?"

"I'm serious."

"So am I."

Brooke stared at him for a brief moment, a smile playing around her mouth at his evasion. "All right. I'll change the subject," she promised, sensing that he was uncomfortable with the compliment.

"Good."

She laughed. "Are you hungry? I could fix some breakfast."

"No, thanks. I usually just have coffee."

"Me too."

"I knew there was a reason I liked you," he teased.

She shook her head slightly and reached into a cupboard for a tray. "It'll just take me a minute to get everything together."

"Can I help?"

"It's not necessary," she said as she moved the sugar, creamer, spoons, and mugs onto the tray. "There's not that much to do."

"Well, I'm here if you change your mind."

"Thanks," she said softly, her eyes watching as the steaming liquid began to drip into the glass pot. "The coffee will be ready soon."

"No rush."

Minutes later, Mark held the tray, while Brooke opened the sliding glass door that led onto the patio.

"I want to thank you for staying. I really appreciate

the company," she said as she stepped out of the house. She moved slightly off to the side, allowing him room to pass her with the tray.

"I'm right next door if you ever need me."

"I know."

"So, are you ever going to get around to telling me just what had you so worked up?" he asked casually, keeping his tone light as he poured the coffee into both mugs.

She shrugged her shoulders slightly. "It was stupid really."

"I doubt it."

Brooke spooned sugar into her coffee and absently ran her finger around the rim of her cup, feeling the little granules of sugar that coated the sides. "I guess my nerves are a little bit on edge."

"That's understandable."

Brooke hesitated a moment longer before admitting, "I really did think someone was in the house."

Mark watched her closely. "I checked all of the rooms. There's nobody here. You're safe."

"I know. Realistically, I know that," she said, before glancing over to the sliding glass doors to where she could see Jake's massive bulk laying on the floor. "I have no doubt that if there was someone actually in the house, Jake would have let me know."

Mark followed her gaze. "I agree. And I'm quite sure he wouldn't have let anyone hurt you."

"I know."

"But?"

"But, it still threw me. With everything going on lately, I'm afraid that I haven't really been thinking that clearly."

Mark took a sip of his coffee as understanding dawned. "You still haven't come to terms with Rick's death," he said, his words a statement and not a question.

"No, I haven't. And I think my conversation with Sharon Millstone yesterday bothered me."

"She called you?" Mark asked, recalling Brooke mentioning her name the day they found the body.

"Yes. She called to see how I was holding up."

"Did she say anything?"

Brooke shrugged. "She mentioned how shocked she and her brother were by the news of Rick's death. Apparently, they had dinner with him just last week."

"They were close?"

"Very."

"Did she say anything else?" Mark asked, curious if there was anything there that might shed some light on the investigation.

"No. Only that Rick was doing really well. His law practice was flourishing and his personal life was starting to look up."

Mark contemplated her words. "Did she expand on her comment about his personal life?"

"What do you mean?"

"She said that his personal life was looking up. Did she happen to mention in what respect?"

"No. I just assumed that she meant that he was starting to see someone romantically."

Mark nodded. "I take it the woman wasn't with him at dinner."

Brooke smiled. "I doubt it. I'm sure I would have received more details if that was the case."

"Why?"

"Because before I started seeing Rick, Sharon dated him."

Chapter Eleven

Mark stilled at her words. "What?"

"Before I met Rick, Sharon dated him."

"She set you up with her old boyfriend?"

Brooke smiled at the surprise evident in Mark's words, in his facial expression. "Yes. You sound shocked."

"You have to admit, that's not something you hear about every day."

"No, it's not."

He looked at her curiously. "Why didn't you mention this earlier?" he asked, knowing that she was usually forthcoming with things of this nature. Brooke liked to share things with him. Little or significant, it didn't seem to matter.

"I guess I didn't think it was relevant," she admitted.

Mark contemplated her across the expanse of the table, watching as her finger absently traced out a pattern on the glass tabletop. Her words were at odds with what he knew about her. Relevance had never entered into their conversations in the past. "How long of a period did Sharon and Rick date for?"

"Not long. I think only a few months. Why?"

Mark shrugged. "No reason. Just curious," he said, not wanting to reveal to her that there might be something to Sharon Millstone's and Rick Cory's relationship that was worth investigating. The circumstances of Brooke's setup with the man were unusual to say the least. He didn't know of many women that would be willing to set up one of their friends with an ex-boyfriend.

"You don't think that she could have somehow been involved in his death, do you?" she asked, following his train of thought.

Mark didn't respond directly to her question. He couldn't afford to. The investigation was still wide open. "There's nothing to suggest it," he hedged. He couldn't forget that Brooke herself was a possible suspect, just based on her actions on the boat. Based on her past association with the victim.

"I've known Sharon a long time. She's always been a good friend," she told him softly. "She's not capable of hurting anyone."

"I'm sure she's not," Mark responded, biting back the words that everybody was capable of hurting someone, given the right incentive. He didn't want to get into a debate with her. Brooke's world seemed more sheltered than his. He didn't want to say anything to her that would put her on guard, anything that she might repeat when she was talking to people. "Let me ask you something."

"What?"

"You didn't find it just the little bit unusual that she introduced you to her old boyfriend?" he asked, sincerely interested in her reply. It would give him an idea of her mindset. An idea of her thought pattern.

She didn't even have to think about her response. It came naturally, and with no hesitation. "No, I didn't. Rick and Sharon were over long before I came on to the scene."

"Without reservations?"

"Without reservations."

Mark nodded. "I take it they remained friends?" he asked, thinking that there had to be some sort of tie between the two of them for their association to continue.

"Good friends."

"Just out of curiosity, who was responsible for their actual breakup?" he asked, taking a sip of his coffee.

Brooke cupped her chin in her palm as she looked across the table, her elbow resting on the glass top. "To be honest, I'm not really sure. I do know that the breakup wasn't bitter, at least on Sharon's part."

"You sound sure of that."

"Nothing was ever said to me that would have hinted otherwise."

"Was she forthcoming on things of that nature?"

"Her personal life?" she asked, considering his question. "I would say so. She wasn't shy about talking, anyway."

"And Rick?"

"What about him?"

"Did he ever talk about his relationship with Sharon with you?"

"No, that wasn't high on our list of conversation topics," she replied wryly.

Mark smiled at her words, knowing that past romantic involvements wouldn't be high on anybody's list. "Sharon didn't happen to mention who the new woman was in Rick's life, did she?"

"No, but to be honest, I didn't ask. My life with Rick was over. And while I wouldn't wish him bad luck in any way, shape, or form, I wasn't quite as understanding as Sharon was when our relationship ended. I don't really think I would have wanted to hear about his new girlfriend."

"I guess that's understandable."

Brooke reached for her cup of coffee, cradling it in both hands. "You know, you never told me whether or not you found out anything that's going to help with Rick's murder investigation."

Mark shrugged. "We didn't find much."

"Would you tell me if you did?" she questioned, trying to gauge his sincerity.

"I would tell you anything that was relevant," he said, his thoughts going back to the earring he found on the boat. The fact that he found one identical to it on Brooke's dresser bothered him. It meant that she couldn't be excluded as a suspect in Rick Cory's murder. But before he mentioned anything to her, before he started to grill her about the location of where the earring was found, he needed to find something else to tie her into the murder.

"You seem quiet all of a sudden," she said.

Mark glanced at her with a small smile. "Sorry. Just tired I guess."

"Me too."

Mark reached for his mug and drained the remainder

of the contents in one swallow. "Are you going to try and get some sleep?"

"Are you?" she countered.

"We both know that's not an easy commodity to come by."

"I know. And it doesn't look like the problem is going to magically disappear."

"Well, there's a lot going on right now," he said, wondering if there might be something else that would explain her bout of insomnia on the morning they found Rick's body floating in the waves. Something that might have to do with the murder itself.

She nodded in agreement to his statement, totally oblivious to his thoughts. "I'd like to thank you for coming over. I appreciate the fact that you came to check on me."

"I'm right next door if you ever need me for anything. If you ever need to talk to someone."

"I know," she said before her eyes caught sight of something on the ground.

Mark followed her gaze. "What is it?" he asked, searching to see what had captured her attention.

"I'm not sure." Brooke rose from her chair and moved over to the object. She bent down as she got closer, her hand reaching for it.

"What did you find?"

"My earring," she said, holding up the small gold hoop triumphantly.

Chapter Twelve

Later that morning, Mark sat in his office. He was busy scanning a report on Brooke Jennings.

He had requested the background check yesterday, after finding her on board Rick Cory's boat. He couldn't deny that he was curious about what it would say. He needed to see if there was anything in the report that would connect her to the man's murder. Her relationship with Cory was too close, and her appearing on the man's boat was something he couldn't ignore. And as much as he liked her, as much as he wanted to believe that she had nothing to do with the man's death, he knew that he couldn't just overlook her association with Cory, or the fact that she had trespassed on a potential crime scene.

He was in the process of reading the final page of the report when there was a knock on his door. Looking up, he saw Walt standing on the other side of the glass. He waved him in.

"Hey," Walt said as he walked into the office and

closed the door behind him. His standard morning fare of a can of soda rested in his hand.

"Morning," Mark returned, closing the report he was reading and placing the file on his desk.

"Am I interrupting anything?"

"No. I was just reading."

"Anything interesting?" Walt asked, motioning to the manila folder.

Mark shrugged. "Not really."

"Who's it on? The floater?"

"No. Brooke Jennings."

Walt looked at him in stunned surprise. "Brooke?"

"Yeah. I wanted to get a better feel for her," Mark told him, not offering any further explanation for his actions, not feeling that he had to.

"What brought this on?" Walt asked when Mark didn't seem inclined to offer any further details. He was curious about what could have caused Mark to run an investigative report on her. Based on the way he protected her, it was the last thing he would have expected.

Mark reached for his coffee mug and took a sip. "The fact that she was on Cory's boat yesterday."

"I was wondering if you were going to act on that. I have to tell you, that was a little suspicious."

Mark inclined his head at Walt's words. He couldn't deny the truth behind them. "Yeah, it was. But I have to be honest. My gut is telling me that she had nothing to do with the murder."

"And the reason you're making that assumption is . . ." Walt prompted when Mark didn't elaborate on his statement.

"Because of the earring," Mark said, picking up the

small plastic bag that contained the earring from his desk. He had held the evidence, wanting to see if he could positively identify it as Brooke's. But now that he confirmed it wasn't hers, he needed to get it to the lab so that it could be tested for trace evidence.

Walt frowned. "I don't understand. You said Brooke has a pair exactly like it."

"The key word is *pair*."

"What?"

"Pair, as in two. She has both earrings in her possession," Mark told him, effectively putting an end to Walt's speculations.

"Two," Walt repeated.

"Yep."

"How common do you think this style is?" Walt asked, motioning with his chin to the gold hoop.

"At a guess, very common."

Walt expelled a breath. "So that means that there was another woman on board the boat."

"It would appear that way."

Walt shook his head in disbelief. "I can't believe that our original team of investigators didn't find this when they were on board that boat. But then, I don't know why it should surprise me. After all, they missed finding that compartment in the paneling."

"The search was sloppy. I've already filed the necessary paperwork writing up the incident," Mark said.

"You wasted no time."

"No, I didn't. We can't afford mistakes like this."

"No, we can't, but can I ask you something?"

"Sure."

"Did you ever consider the possibility that Brooke

pointed out that compartment to us yesterday because she was trapped?"

"Trapped? You mean because we walked in on her?"

"Yes."

Mark steepled his hands near his mouth as he considered Walt's words. "Why would she have done that?" he asked, playing devil's advocate.

"Maybe she was there to clean up the rest of the mess. Maybe there was something in that compartment that she was after. Something that would explain how the blood became present."

"If that was the case, why would she point it out to us like she did? Why not pretend that she didn't know anything about it?"

"Maybe she was trying to lead the investigation away from her."

"Until yesterday, she had no clue that she was even part of the investigation," Mark reminded him.

Walt looked doubtful. "She's not naïve. She could have put two and two together and come up with four. She had to know that her association with the murder victim would bring their relationship under scrutiny."

"Yes. But it was her presence on board the boat that really put the spotlight on her. If she had managed to get off the boat undetected, we wouldn't even be having this conversation right now."

"True," Walt acknowledged. "Was there anything in that report that would substantiate the theory that she was involved with the murder?"

"No," Mark said, glancing at the file on his desk and recalling the contents. He had been somewhat surprised at how sparse the report was.

"So, how do we proceed?" Walt asked.

"Right now, we have this earring to contend with."

"This definitely puts a new twist on things, especially if it was left by the murderer."

"I know. I'm waiting for the report to come back on the blood found in the compartment. Hopefully, there will be something there that will be of help. We should at least be able to identify whether or not the blood was Rick Cory's."

Walt glanced at his watch. "When do you expect to have the report?"

"It should be here any moment," Mark said just as he noticed Megan Smith coming toward his office. "This may be it now."

Walt turned to see who was coming. A smile of greeting crossed his face as Megan knocked on the office door and entered.

"Hi," she said.

"Good morning, Megan," Mark replied.

She turned to Walt with a smile. "Morning," she said before walking closer to Mark's desk. "Here's the report that you wanted."

Mark took the file. "Thanks. Did we come up with anything?"

She shrugged. "I don't know. I'm not the one who did the actual testing. They only asked me to bring the file because I had to come in this direction anyway. To be honest, I didn't even glance at the report."

Walt looked over at her with a knowing smile. "Are you on a donut run?" he asked, making a reference to the box of fresh donuts that was always by the coffee machine.

"Got it in one," she replied with a laugh.

Mark smiled. "Well, don't let me keep you."

"You're not." Then her eyes caught sight of the small gold hoop in the protective bag on his desk. She reached for it. "Hey," she exclaimed excitedly. "You found my earring."

Chapter Thirteen

Mark stilled. "Your earring?"

Megan didn't notice the effect her words had. "Yes. I've been looking all over for it."

Mark's eyes narrowed slightly as he contemplated her. Kicking his chair back from his desk, he stretched his legs out in front of him. "When did you lose it?"

"When did I lose it?" she repeated.

"Yeah. You must have some idea," he replied, watching her body language, searching her facial expression. Her words had thrown him. While he acknowledged that the forensics team had not done a wonderful job in securing the evidence from the boat, he hadn't thought to include Megan with that group. She was too committed to her profession. She had too much of a personal stake in solving the cases. It was what drove her. It's what gave her the ambition to succeed at her chosen career.

Megan took a moment to think. "I think I lost it the day you found the body of the guy floating in the Atlantic."

"Are you sure?" Mark asked.

"Not a hundred percent."

"How about reasonably?"

"That would be a fair assessment."

Mark inclined his head at her words. "Were you on the team that went to the boat to perform the search?"

"No. Why?"

Mark motioned to the earring. "That's where that was found."

"Really?" she asked, her voice betraying her shock at the news.

"Yes."

Megan shook her head and placed the earring back on the desk. "Then it can't be mine. I was nowhere near the boat."

"Do you think it's possible that you dropped it on the beach when you were working?" Walt asked.

"I suppose it's possible," she said with a shrug.

Walt looked over at Mark. "Maybe one of the other technicians picked it up at the beach and accidentally dropped it on the boat."

Megan looked at both men. "I doubt it. The earring design is very common. It could belong to anyone."

Mark nodded in resignation. "I had an idea that would be the case."

"If you'd like, I'll take it with me and see if we can find anything on it in the lab."

"I was going to drop it off later, myself. If you can take it now, you'll save me a trip," Mark said.

"Not a problem."

Walt was watching her. "Just out of curiosity, what do you expect to find on the earring?"

Megan looked down at the small golden object. "I don't know. I imagine it's possible that there may be some blood present."

"Why would there be blood on it?" Mark asked.

"It's possible that the woman who wore it might have had a problem with her earlobe."

"That happens?" Walt asked with surprise as he thought of his wife and the large, heavy earrings she wore religiously. She had never once complained about a problem.

"Yes," Megan said. "Not frequently, but it's not unheard of. There's also the possibility that there was some type of force applied to the earlobe that forced the earring post out of the piercing."

Walt thought about the hair he found entangled in the watch of the victim. "If a strand of hair was snagged in the earring, and then that same strand of hair was caught in a watch strap, would that be enough force to remove the earring?"

"Definitely. The catch on an earring isn't that secure," Megan replied. She paused for a brief moment before asking, "Why? Are you thinking there might be some connection to the strand of hair you found attached to Rick Cory's watch?"

"Yeah."

Megan glanced at Mark. "It is possible."

"I know. But I found the earring in the cabin, not up on deck where we suspect the murder may have taken place."

"There's always the possibility that it was brought

into the cabin by one of our guys. Or it could just be that it wound up there purely by chance. It's not heavy. If Cory did pull it out of a woman's earlobe, maybe the force of the movement sent it flying into the cabin," Walt said.

Mark stared at Walt for a brief moment before redirecting his attention to Megan. "How soon before you know if there's any trace evidence?"

"Sometime today. The test is relatively simple."

Mark nodded slightly. "Get back with me as soon as you can regarding the results."

"Not a problem," she said as she took the bag and walked to the door. She paused with her hand on the knob. "You know, there is another possibility of how this came to be on board the boat."

"What's that?" Walt asked.

"It could belong to the victim," she said.

"But he was a guy," Walt said.

Megan looked over at Walt, one eyebrow raised. "So? Men have been known to wear earrings. If I were you, I would check the autopsy report. Maybe the pathologist noted it," she said just before she turned and walked out of the room.

Walt watched her go before turning to Mark. "Do you think there's a possibility that the earring belonged to Cory?"

Mark shrugged and reached for the file that contained the autopsy report. "There's only one way to find out."

Walt drummed his fingers on the arm of his chair as he waited for Mark to scan the report. "Well?"

Mark sighed. "He had his right ear pierced."

Walt reached for his now lukewarm soda and took a sip. "That means that it could belong to him."

"It could."

"What about the report on the blood we found on board the boat?"

Mark opened the file that Megan had just brought, and leaned back in his chair to read the data.

"Well?"

"The DNA in the sample is a match for Rick Cory," Mark said, before shifting his attention back to the autopsy report. "And there's a notation about a cut to his right hand. According to the examiner, the cut had almost healed."

Walt digested the information. "The amount of blood we found wasn't excessive. If it matches Cory's, we'll just have to assume that the blood left in the safe had nothing to do with the man's murder."

"I agree."

Walt was silent for a moment before saying, "We don't even know for sure if the murder was actually committed on Cory's boat."

"But it's the best guess so far," Mark said, focusing his attention back to the latest report. He flipped the page and scanned the second page.

"Any prints?" Walt asked.

"No."

"So we have nothing to take to the bank."

Mark closed the file and pushed it in Walt's direction so that he could look at the document. "Not in there anyway."

Walt picked up the report, scanning the data. "So where do you want to go from here?"

Mark shrugged. "I'd like to find out a little bit more about the victim. The background report was kind of vague. And even with the information Brooke was able to tell me, there are still a lot of open holes in the guy's history."

"Yeah, I know what you mean."

"Obviously the man had money, but I'm not sure his law practice would support his lifestyle. The life he was living would demand a fairly hefty bankroll."

"Family money?" Walt asked.

Mark picked up Cory's background report. "There's nothing here pointing in that direction. Both of his parents are deceased. His father was an attorney, but his practice didn't appear to be lucrative. From a business standpoint, there was nothing there."

Walt kicked his long legs out before him, relaxing fully in his chair. "No record trails from Cory's bank?"

"No."

"And no criminal record was noted," Walt said, thinking aloud.

"We ran his prints, he came back clean."

"No aliases?"

"Not that we know of. At least if there were, he was never arrested under any of them," Mark said.

"So, basically he's a blank slate."

"That pretty much sums it up. With the exception of what Brooke has been able to tell me, and the limited information in his background report."

Walt drained the remainder of his can in one gulp. "All that information," he said as he gestured to the files fanned out on Mark's desk, "and none of it helpful."

"There's nothing that's standing out as of yet."

"Everything's back that we were waiting for?"

"It's all here," Mark said as he tapped a pen on the folders. "A few of the reports were late getting in, but they're all here now."

"Was anything there that might be useful?"

"Maybe. At least at first glance."

"What do you mean?"

"One of the reports that was late was on Brooke's friend Sharon Millstone."

"So?"

"The woman dated Rick Cory. She was also responsible for setting the guy up with Brooke," Mark said.

"That might not mean anything."

"I know. But it's worth investigating."

Walt nodded absently, agreeing with him. "I thought for sure we would have something concrete by now."

"Yeah, me too." Mark understood Walt's aggravation. Ideally, they should have had some physical evidence to go on by now. It was amazing really that Cory's background was so clean. Normally you could count on there being at least one skeleton in the closet, something that would at least give you a glimpse as to the reasoning behind the crime. This time, they seemed to come up against a brick wall.

"How do you want to proceed?" Walt asked.

Mark rocked back in his chair, swiveling it slightly as he contemplated Walt. "Actually, I thought we could try and talk to Cory's neighbors."

"The uniforms didn't do that?"

"The guy's primary residence is listed as one of the high-rise buildings on the ocean. In the penthouse to be exact. There weren't many people around that day for the officers to talk to, and there was nothing to demand that somebody be posted outside the building to question everybody that came through the lobby."

"You think we'll have better luck today?"

Mark shrugged. "I'm not sure. It's worth a shot."

"I'm willing to give anything a try."

"I also wanted to check out the people Brooke mentioned to me that have a connection with our victim."

"Sure. Who are they?"

"Sharon Millstone, the woman I just mentioned to you, her brother Evan Millstone, and Marissa James. It was their background reports that were late coming in."

"What's Evan Millstone's relationship to the victim?" Walt asked.

"Sharon Millstone and her brother, Evan Millstone, are the ones who introduced Brooke to Cory."

"Do we have any other information on them?"

"Sharon is a schoolteacher at the same school Brooke works at, and her brother is a lawyer who used to work at the same firm as Cory. And like I said, Sharon Millstone has a connection to the man in more than a casual sense."

"And Marissa James?"

"Cory's secretary. Apparently, she's very loyal. She followed him to his own practice after he left the firm they were both working at."

"It sounds like she's dedicated."

"It looks that way, but we both know appearances can be deceiving," Mark responded.

"Didn't the guy have an ex-wife somewhere?" Walt asked.

"Yeah. Her name is Randy. She has an alibi for the night of the murder."

"What is it?"

"She's in England with her husband on business. She has been for the last two weeks," Mark said.

"Are you sure that she didn't return to the States?"

"Positive."

"Well, maybe something will come up with the other three people you mentioned."

"That's what I'm hoping for."

"When did you want to leave?"

Mark glanced at his watch. "I have a meeting in about an hour. I'll have to wait until that's over before we can go."

"Not a problem. I have some paperwork to finish. That should keep me busy," Walt said as he rose from his chair and stretched his legs. "Give a shout when you're ready."

"Count on it."

Chapter Fourteen

A couple of hours later, Mark and Walt were in Evan Millstone's office, waiting for the man to put in an appearance. Mark found himself by the glass-paned wall that offered an unobstructed view of the outside grounds, while Walt walked around the room curiously.

"The guy has a nice office," Walt casually commented, his eyes taking in the glass top modern desk and built-in bookcases. They blended with the contemporary feel of the suite of offices in the three-story professional building.

"It's okay," Mark said, preoccupied. "Are you sure the guy knew what time to expect us?" He knew Walt called to arrange the meeting about an hour before.

"Positive. He said he would be in all day. Besides, his secretary showed us into his office. She wouldn't have done that if he wasn't here."

Mark looked at the small clock on the desk.

"We've been here fifteen minutes already," he said impatiently.

"Relax. Give the man some time. When I explained to him that we wanted to talk to him, he gave the impression that he was willing to cooperate."

"What was your feeling on him when you had him on the phone?"

Walt thought about his conversation with Evan Millstone. "There was nothing there that shouted he had something to hide. He sounded like he wanted the chance to help solve Cory's murder."

"Did he open up on the phone at all?"

"Not much."

"Did he mention how long they knew each other for?"

"Nothing concrete. He just said that they both went to law school together," Walt replied.

"There should be some history there if they've known each other for that length of time."

"I agree. He also volunteered to have his sister join us here. Maybe that's to show a good faith effort on their part that they're both willing to help with Cory's murder investigation."

"Maybe. But there's a greater probability that it's because he didn't want us questioning her without him being present," Mark pointed out, thinking that the guy had a general idea that his sister might be considered as having a possible motive for Cory's murder.

"You might be right. I know having them both here at the same time makes our life easier, but it might have been better to interview them each individually. It would give us a better reading on the two."

"I know. But there's really no way to force it. If we called Sharon Millstone in for formal questioning, she would have the right to an attorney anyway. And her brother would probably be her legal counsel of choice."

"True. But this type of meeting gives them both the opportunity to field each other's responses. I think it's a safe bet that Evan Millstone isn't going to let his sister say anything incriminating."

"That's a given."

"We'll just have to see how this plays out," Walt said just as the door to the office opened and two people walked into the room.

Mark immediately walked toward them. "Evan Millstone?"

Evan Millstone inclined his head and reached out a hand to Mark. "Yes. Police Chief, Tanner, isn't it?"

Mark shook the man's outstretched hand. "Yes. This is Detective Walt Tyler," he said, introducing Walt who stood by his side.

Evan Millstone shook Walt's hand before introducing the woman who stood beside him. "This is my sister, Sharon. Please have a seat," he said, gesturing to the two chairs in front of the desk.

"I appreciate you taking the time to speak with us," Mark began, his eyes sweeping over Sharon Millstone, noting her blond hair. The shade looked like it might match the strand snagged on Cory's watch.

Evan Millstone seated his sister at a chair on the side of the desk before taking his place behind it. "It's not a problem. I understand the nature of this meeting is regarding Rick Cory's murder."

"Yes," Mark replied. "I need to know what you can tell me about the man. I understand you were both friends of his."

"That's right. My sister, Sharon, even dated him for a while," Evan Millstone said quietly, without hesitation.

Mark kept his expression neutral as he turned slightly to look at Sharon Millstone. "I'm sorry for your loss," he said sincerely, trying to judge her reaction to the words.

"Thank you," she replied, her voice low and soft with the thickness of tears just below the surface. "Rick was a good friend."

"I'm sure he was. If you don't mind my asking, how long ago did you break up?"

"About three and a half years ago. But it was a mutual breakup. There were no hard feelings."

"How long did you date him?" Walt asked.

"Not long at all. Maybe two months," she admitted, taking a moment to reflect on it. "I had met him through Evan."

"At the office?" Mark asked.

"No. At a dinner party at Evan's house. It was an evening where there were too many lawyers present, and too much conversation about caseloads," she said, her eyes reflecting her sadness at Cory's death as she recalled the evening. "I was sitting out on the verandah when Rick came out to get some air. We started talking and thought it would be nice to get to know one another. Things just sort of progressed from there. But it didn't take long for us to realize that we had no real common ground to base a relationship on. So we became friends. Good friends," she said, pausing for a moment before admitting, "I even introduced him to Brooke Jennings, a friend of mine. I thought that they would make a nice couple."

"I know Brooke," Mark admitted.

Sharon looked at Mark with surprise. "Really?"

"She's my neighbor."

"She's a very nice person. I really thought her and Rick would be together forever."

Mark didn't respond to her comment. There was nothing to say. "Do you know if Rick was dating anyone else?"

"Recently?" Evan asked, trying to get clarification on the question on his sister's behalf.

Mark glanced at him. "Yes. Was he seeing anyone that you were aware of? Anyone that we should know about that might help us with the investigation on his death?"

"We had dinner with him last week. He hinted about a possible relationship," Evan admitted.

"Just hinted? Nothing more specific?"

Evan smiled sadly. "Not anything concrete. After Brooke, Rick began playing the field a little bit. I don't think he wanted to get seriously involved with another woman. They had seen each other too long, and I think he just wanted to take things easy. His breakup with Brooke took a toll on Rick. When Sharon said that she thought they would be together forever, I think Rick thought the same way. There were many nights after their breakup that I saw him out on the town with different women, but I honestly couldn't say whether or not he felt serious about any one of them. From outward appearances, I would have to say no. So when he mentioned this woman last week, I really didn't pay that much attention to it. I figured he was just testing the waters again, so to speak."

"But Brooke and Rick parted as friends?" Walt asked.

Sharon fielded that question. "As far as I know. At the very least, they parted on good terms. Their breakup was a mutual decision."

Mark nodded slightly at her response and looked at Evan. "Did he have any enemies that you were aware of?"

Evan shifted in his chair and lifted a shoulder in a shrug. "He practiced criminal law. I'm afraid that goes with the territory. If you're asking if I can think of anyone that would want to kill him, then my answer would have to be no. But then again, I'm not familiar with his current and past caseloads. The only time our paths crossed at the courthouse was on the outside steps."

"What about his secretary?" Mark asked.

"Marissa James?" Evan questioned.

"Yes. What can you tell me about her?"

Evan leaned back in his chair and steepled his hands together on the desktop. "Marissa used to work for my firm before Rick branched out on his own."

"Was she close to Rick?"

"Professionally, I don't think someone could have gotten closer. From the moment they were introduced, they formed an instant bond. Marissa always seemed to be able to anticipate Rick's needs regarding cases that he represented."

"And personally?" Walt asked.

"Personally, I think Marissa wanted more, but I don't think Rick thought of her in that regard."

"How did she take that emotionally?" Mark asked, wondering if there might be something to that statement. He was well aware that once emotions got involved, common sense and reality often fell by the wayside.

Evan shrugged. "She worked for the man for over twelve years. I would say that she learned to cope."

"Working somewhere for twelve years is unusual in today's day and age," Walt said.

"Yes, it is," Evan agreed. "Marissa was very loyal to Rick. That's why I really believe she came to accept that they would never be anything other than friends and associates. If she did have a problem with their relationship, she did a great job of covering up the fact."

"How is she handling the news of Cory's death?" Walt asked.

"Not well at all," Evan replied honestly. "To be blunt, she's devastated. But when you work with someone as closely as she worked with Rick, that's to be expected."

"Is Rick's law office open right now?" Mark asked.

Evan nodded. "He had a junior associate that's holding down the fort. But I would imagine that eventually, all of his clients will have to find alternate legal representation. The person standing in for Rick doesn't have the experience to handle the caseload."

"Do you know if Marissa James is working now? Or if she's taking some time off?" Walt asked.

"I can't be sure, but I think she's working. I saw her on the courthouse steps when I drove to work this morning. She looked dressed for the office. If you'd like, I can call her on her cell phone and ask if she has the time to meet with you this afternoon."

"If you could, that would be very helpful," Mark said.

"Sure," Evan replied as he reached for his phone and dialed a number. After a minute of conversation, he hung up and looked at Mark. "She said she'll be back at Rick's office within twenty minutes. Her calendar is clear for the rest of the afternoon, so if you want to head over there, she'll be happy to talk to you."

Mark inclined his head. "Thanks."

"It wasn't a problem. Are there any other questions that my sister or I could answer for you?"

Mark stood. "Not right now. Thank you for your time though. I appreciate all your help."

Evan rose from his chair to walk Mark and Walt to the door. "It's nothing. My sister and I want to help in any way we can with the investigation. Please call me if you have any further questions."

"I will. Thanks," Mark said before shaking Evan's hand and leaving the office. He turned to Walt as soon as the door closed behind them. "Let's head over to Cory's office."

"Sure," Walt said, walking beside Mark to the outside entrance of the building. "So what did you think?"

"About Evan Millstone and Sharon Millstone?"

"Yeah. What was your impression?"

"I don't think they were trying to hide anything. Their responses didn't seem guarded anyway."

"I didn't think so either."

"I was a little surprised by the revelation that Marissa James possibly wanted a relationship with the guy in a way other than professional," Mark said.

"There might be a motive there."

"I was thinking the same thing. It'll be interesting to see how she handles herself in our presence."

Walt was silent for a moment before saying, "Yeah, it will. But you know, I think we can definitely rule out Sharon Millstone as a possible suspect."

"Why do you say that?"

"If Sharon Millstone had any hard feelings toward the guy, she would have made it known sometime during Rick and Brooke's courtship. And based on what she told us, that didn't seem to be the case."

"No, it didn't. I didn't pick up on any potential problems she may have had with the man or his relationship with Brooke. She freely admitted that things just didn't work out between the two of them. But that doesn't mean that I'm willing to write her off as a possible suspect."

"You think it was a little strange that she introduced Cory to Brooke?" Walt asked.

"It's unconventional considering the fact that she dated the guy. But if Sharon Millstone ended her relationship with Rick Cory on amicable terms, it could be that she just wanted to see the guy happy."

Walt was silent for a moment before he suggested, "We don't have anybody to confirm exactly how the relationship ended."

"Just Sharon Millstone's word. But the investigation

is still open. There's always the chance that something else will come up."

"True."

"So let's go see if we can find it."

Chapter Fifteen

Mark and Walt walked the few short blocks to Cory's office. The Florida sun was scorching, and Walt hooked his suit jacket over his shoulder as he tried to find some measure of relief. He glanced in Mark's direction. "You're not hot?"

Mark looked over at him with a raised eyebrow, an incredulous expression on his face. "It's ninety-five degrees according to the temperature display at the bank we just passed. Of course I'm hot."

Walt shrugged. "I was just curious. You don't look too uncomfortable."

"That's probably because my mind is on Marissa James."

"Oh?"

Mark adjusted his sunglasses. "The more I think about her relationship with Cory, the more questions I have."

"What do you mean?"

"I mean, if Evan Millstone was right, and Marissa James wanted more from her relationship with Cory than he was willing to give, why was her attachment and loyalty to him so strong?"

"Maybe she's a realist and was willing to accept the only type of relationship he could offer."

"At the cost of her pride and self esteem?" Mark asked doubtfully.

"Stranger things have been known to happen," Walt reminded him. "You know as well as I do that people stay together for all sorts of reasons. Some make sense, and others don't. Everybody's needs and expectations are different. If the only time she could spend with Cory was in a professional manner, maybe that was enough for her."

"Maybe. But something just doesn't add up. If the woman actually had a thing for Cory, I'm not quite sure she would have stuck with him through his other relationships. That would have had to be rough on her. To want something, and know that it's beyond your reach."

"What are you getting at?" Walt asked, as they came to a street corner and waited for the traffic light to turn.

"What if she stayed with Cory because she knew his other relationships were doomed from failure at the onset? By all indications, she spent a lot of time in Cory's presence. She had to have some sort of handle on what he was looking for in a relationship."

"You think she was biding her time with the expectation that Cory would suddenly feel different toward her eventually?"

"It's something to consider. If she was as loyal to Cory as what we're led to believe, you have to also make the assumption that they were friends. Maybe she was feeling him out, waiting for him to take notice of her as something more than a friend or employee," Mark said.

"We can't discard the notion that according to his friends, there was never anything there."

"True, but we also can't discard the notion that based on that fact, she may have been setting him up for the ultimate revenge. If Marissa James' feelings for Cory were strong enough, she may have felt some sort of betrayal from him for not returning her feelings."

"You think by her being a shoulder for him to lean on when his other relationships went bad, that she may have somehow made a place for herself in his life that would allow her the opportunity to get revenge."

"I do," Mark said, just as a white convertible pulled to a stop in front of the building they were heading to. A woman stepped out of the vehicle, automatically reaching into the back seat for a briefcase. She casually glanced their way as they approached her.

"Police Chief Tanner, isn't it?" she asked, waiting until they reached her side.

"That's right," Mark said, stopping in front of the woman, his eyes taking in everything about her appearance from the conservative business suit, to the auburn hair elegantly piled on top of her head. "Have we met before?" he asked, unable to place her.

She shook her head slightly. "Not formally, but I've seen your picture in the paper. I'm Marissa James. Evan Millstone told me to expect you."

Mark carefully kept his expression neutral as he reached out to shake her hand. "It's a pleasure to meet you, though I am sorry it's under these circumstances." He turned to Walt. "This is Detective Walt Tyler."

Marissa shook his hand before motioning toward the building. "Why don't we go inside where we'll have some privacy."

"I appreciate your taking the time to talk to us," Mark said as he followed her into the darkened corridor that led to the entryway.

"I'll do anything I can to help find Rick's killer," she assured him softly, her breath catching slightly on her words. After unlocking a door, she ushered both Mark and Walt into an office. "Please, have a seat."

"Thanks," Mark said, both him and Walt waiting until she sat down behind the desk before taking their own seats.

Marissa reached for a tissue as soon as she sat down. "I'm sorry about this," she apologized as she dabbed at tears.

"There's no need to apologize," Mark said. "If you need a few minutes to get yourself together . . ."

"No, that's okay, I'll be fine," she said, crumbling the tissue in her hand. "You spoke to Evan and Sharon Millstone today?"

"That's right."

"They were good friends of Rick's. We were all shocked by the news."

"It's hard to make sense of something like this," Mark agreed. "That's why I think it's important that we talk to you. On a professional level, you seemed very close to Rick Cory. Is there anyone that you know of who may have threatened him recently? Any cases that he was working on where someone may have held a grudge against him?"

Marissa was shaking her head before Mark stopped speaking. "No. There was no one that I know of that would have been capable of killing him."

"How about someone in his past?"

Marissa shifted slightly in her chair as she leaned back against the cushion. "I'm sure you heard about Ellen Manning."

"Yes."

"To the best of my knowledge, she was the only person who would have hurt Rick. She devastated him when the gun she fired killed his son."

"She's still in prison," Mark assured her.

Marissa nodded. "I know. I checked into it after I heard about Rick's death."

Mark was surprised by her statement, but was careful to keep it from showing. "I guess it pays to have connections."

"Yes, it does," she replied in all seriousness before realizing that she should explain her actions. "Please understand, when I heard of Rick's death, Ellen Manning was the first person that popped into my mind as having a motive. I needed to reassure myself that she was still locked up."

"That's reasonable," Mark said, knowing that the woman's close relationship with Rick played a big factor in her actions. "Is there anyone else you could think of other than Ellen Manning that may have had a problem with Rick?"

"No," she replied without hesitation.

"Was Rick seeing anybody?" Walt asked.

"Seeing anybody? You mean like dating?"

"That's right," Walt replied.

"Not anyone special. He was dating a woman by the name of Brooke Jennings for a couple of years. After their breakup, he seemed to want to distance himself from any personal involvement for a while."

"What do you mean by personal involvement?" Mark asked.

She shrugged slightly. "Any relationships that had any substance. Any relationship that would demand emotional payment from him. He began to date casually, and only people that had no expectations from him."

"Ones that he could turn away without any hard feelings on either side?" Walt asked in an attempt to clarify her meaning.

"Exactly."

"Was there anyone he was seeing that might have expected more from him than he was willing to give?" Mark asked.

"None that I could pinpoint. Rick and I were friends, but he was never the type to kiss and tell. And he very rarely merged his personal life with his business life. I've worked with the man for twelve years, and it was only recently that I was invited onto his boat."

Her words gave Mark pause. "How long ago were you on the boat?"

"A couple of weeks ago. Why?"

"No reason. Did you like sailing?"

She grimaced slightly. "We never made it out of the marina."

"Why?"

"I get seasick," she admitted.

Walt smiled slightly. "You have my sympathy."

She looked over at Mark and Walt, her gaze encompassing both men. "I wish I could tell you something that would assist with the investigation, but I'm afraid I don't know which direction to point you in."

"You've been very helpful," Mark said before reaching inside his suit pocket for a business card. He held it out to her. "If you can think of anything else, please call me."

She reached for the card. "I will."

Mark stood to his feet. "We've taken up enough of your time," he said as Walt joined him.

Marissa stood also. "If you need to talk to me again, my door is open."

"Thanks. I may take you up on that," Mark said before heading toward the door. He waited until Walt closed the door behind him before saying, "She gets seasick."

"So she claims," Walt said.

Mark smiled grimly. "The only way to test it would be to take her out on a boat. Which is something we can't force."

"No, I know," Walt said. "I have to be honest, though. She didn't leave me with the impression that she was totally devastated by Cory's death. Upset yes, but a long way from devastated."

"I agree. The woman's definitely not in mourning. But there's always the possibility that she wasn't as emotionally tied to Cory as everybody believes."

"If that's the case, she sure went out of her way to give everybody a different impression."

"Maybe they only saw what they wanted to see. You have to admit, the very fact that she quit her job to follow him when he opened his own law practice was probably enough for everyone to draw the conclusion that she felt something more than just professional respect."

"Why wouldn't she have felt the need to set the record straight? She had to know what people thought."

"Maybe she doesn't care about other people's opinions," Mark suggested.

"I guess that's a possibility," Walt acknowledged before asking, "Did you notice that her hair color doesn't match the strand we found?"

"Yeah, I did. But that doesn't mean she wasn't involved with the murder. We have nothing concrete to suggest that the hair found in Cory's watch strap was left by the murderer."

"I realize that."

"We don't have enough information to confirm any one theory as of yet."

"True," Walt said, glancing at his watch. "It's getting late and I'm hungry. Do you want to get something to eat before we head over to Cory's condo to talk to his neighbors?"

"Sure, but just something quick. I want to get this over with," Mark said as they began the walk back to the car.

Chapter Sixteen

Later that evening, Mark was on his way home. The sun was just beginning to set, taking away the oppressive heat. The humidity of that afternoon had been unbearable, and the afternoon thunderstorm that you could normally count on didn't take place. The slight drop in temperature was a welcome relief.

He ran a weary hand through his hair as he slowed the car to a stop near a traffic light. As he waited for the light to turn green, he thought about his day. The trip to Rick Cory's residence proved fruitless, none of his neighbors seemed willing to talk about the man. At least that was the impression they gave. Answers to his and Walt's inquiries had been short and vague, shedding absolutely no light on Cory's lifestyle. The result was frustrating. He had honestly thought that the natural curiosity of people would have had them willing to talk, willing to open up. Usually, people didn't need to be coaxed into talking about the deceased. Friend or foe, death had a way of loosening the most reserved person's tongue.

The sudden ringing of his cell phone interrupted his thoughts. "Tanner."

"Mark?"

Mark recognized Walt's voice immediately. "Yeah, Walt. What's up?"

"I just received a call from one of Cory's neighbors. Apparently, the guy just came back into town from a business trip, and he heard that we were asking questions. He said he might have some information that we would find useful."

"When can he meet with us?"

"He's heading toward the station now. Meet me down there?"

"Give me fifteen minutes," Mark said, before disconnecting. He cast a quick glance in his rearview mirror before changing lanes to make the u-turn that led back to the station.

Parking in his reserved spot, he saw Walt standing outside the police precinct talking to Megan. He walked over to them.

"Hi," Mark said.

Walt turned. "Hey. You made good time."

"I wasn't that far away. I take it the guy didn't arrive yet?"

"No. He should be here soon."

Mark nodded and turned to Megan. "Working late again?"

She smiled. "I just finished the report on the earring."

Mark glanced at the file in Walt's hand. "Is that the report?"

"Yeah," Walt said, handing him the file. "I ran into Megan and intercepted it. I was just walking her to her car."

Mark glanced at Megan. "Did you find anything?" he asked, opening the file and beginning to scan the information.

"No. There was no DNA present and no clear fingerprints."

Mark grunted and continued to read the file.

"You guys didn't come across anything else today?" she asked, looking at both Mark and Walt questioningly.

"Not physical evidence," Mark replied, closing the file. "But we may have a lead from one of Cory's neighbors. That's who we came to meet." He turned to Walt. "When did he call?"

"Right before I called you. He said he was coming right over. He should be here soon."

Mark glanced back at Megan and smiled. "I appreciate you staying to complete this report."

"It's not a problem. I was happy to do it. I would have had it done earlier, but we were short-handed today. I'm just sorry that nothing showed."

"So am I."

"If you want me to hang around just in case the guy you're meeting with has something . . ."

"No, but thanks. If something comes in tonight, it'll hold until morning," Mark said.

"I don't mind staying."

"I know. And I appreciate it. But it's getting late. You should head on home."

"All right. But call if you need me to come in."

"I will," Mark said, watching as she walked off to her car. He waited until she was safely inside before he reached for the double glass doors that led to the precinct. "I was really hoping that something would show on the earring."

Walt shrugged. "It could just be that the earring belonged to Rick Cory. We already know that his ear was pierced. And if you think about it, the design of the earring could be used by both men and women. It's pretty generic."

At his office, Mark waited until Walt entered the room before stepping inside. "It seems kind of strange that we have two women who own pairs exactly like it. You would think that a man would purchase something a little simpler in design."

Walt took a seat. "If it did belong to him, who could say what the appeal was. The fact that two women we know own the earring is interesting, but hardly conclusive for any kind of theory."

Mark took his own seat. "I know."

"Maybe the guy just had eccentric taste."

"Maybe. But we still don't have anything solid to go on in this case."

"I know. But hopefully the guy coming here is going to change that."

Mark leaned back in his chair, his thoughts going back to his reason for coming back to the police station. "What did Cory's neighbor say when he called? Did he give any hint as to why he wanted to meet with us?"

"No. He seemed kind of hesitant to speak on the phone."

"That may or may not be relevant," Mark said just as his intercom buzzed. After a few words of conversation, he disconnected the call. "Cory's neighbor is here."

"That was quick," Walt said, rising from his chair. "Do you want to stay here and I'll go and bring him in?"

"Sounds good."

"I'll be right back."

Mark leaned back in his chair as he waited for him to return. It was only a moment later before Walt walked back in.

Mark stood the moment Walt entered the room, his eyes automatically focusing on the middle-aged man beside him.

"Benjamin Jones? This is Police Chief Mark Tanner."

Mark automatically reached out to shake the man's hand. "Mr. Jones. Please, have a seat," he invited, motioning to the chair in front of his desk.

Jones took a seat. "I appreciate you gentlemen taking the time to meet with me."

"It's not a problem," Mark assured him as he took his own seat. "Detective Tyler had mentioned that you called regarding Rick Cory's murder investigation."

Jones ran a restless hand through his black hair that was liberally sprinkled with gray. "That's right. Some of the people who live in my building had mentioned that you were looking for some information pertaining to Rick's death."

"That's correct," Mark replied.

Jones shifted restlessly in his chair. "I think I have some information you'll find useful."

"So I understand," Mark said, curious about the nervous demeanor of the man. While he knew some people were intimidated by law officials, he wasn't quite sure if he would classify this man as one of them. People who contacted the police on their own were usually willing to talk.

"I was out of town all week on business, so I wasn't here when the murder occurred. Otherwise I would have contacted you immediately," Jones said, still procrastinating with the real reason behind his visit.

Mark nodded. "I appreciate that. Right now, we could use all the help we can get."

"I thought that would be the case."

"So, what can you tell us about the man?"

"I wasn't sure if you were aware of the fact that Rick had dated a woman for several years," Jones said.

Mark's eyes narrowed slightly at the man's words and he leaned back in his chair. "Who?" he asked. He didn't want to lead the conversation in any way. He couldn't afford to. It was important that any evidence discovered hold up in court.

"Her name was Brooke Jennings."

"And you think she pertains to this investigation?"

"To be honest, I'm not sure. I saw her with Rick a couple of weeks ago on his boat."

"So?"

"So, they were arguing."

Walt shifted sideways in his chair so that he could see the man's face better. "What makes you so sure that they were arguing?"

Jones lifted one shoulder expressively. "It was obvious by their tone of voices."

"How did you happen to be in a place where you could hear what was being said?" Mark asked.

"I have a sailboat docked two slips down from Rick's. I was on my boat that night. I couldn't help but overhear part of their conversation."

"What was said?" Walt asked.

"I couldn't make out all the words, just a few."

"Can you recall what the words were?" Mark asked.

"I can't be sure, but it sounded as if she threatened him."

Chapter Seventeen

"Threatened?" Mark repeated.

"That's right," Jones replied.

"In what manner?" Walt asked. They couldn't afford to move forward on this case based on speculation. They needed cold hard facts.

Benjamin Jones' gaze encompassed both men. "As I said, I couldn't hear exactly what was said. It was more the tone of voice that I found disturbing."

Mark made eye contact with the man. "You still haven't mentioned exactly what it was that you heard."

Benjamin was silent for a moment before saying, "I thought I heard the words 'it ends tonight.'"

"And it was a female's voice?" Mark asked.

"Yes."

"That's it? That's all you heard?" Walt questioned.

"That's all I could make out."

"How long were you at the marina for?" Mark asked, trying to determine if the man may have heard just parts of a conversation and possibly took the information out of context.

Jones' forehead creased in a frown as he tried to recall the night. "A few hours. I know I was on my boat already when they arrived at Rick's."

"Are you positive?" Walt asked.

"Yes. I was cleaning out the cabin when I heard them walk by."

"So you were below deck," Mark said.

"Yes."

Mark studied the man across his desk. "So, how can you be positive that it was Brooke Jennings with Rick Cory? Did you actually see her face? Did you talk to them?"

"No, I recognized her voice."

"When was the last time you spoke with her that you would have that kind of recollection of her voice?" Mark asked.

"At a party right before her breakup with Rick."

Walt looked at the man curiously. "Where was the party?"

"On Rick's sailboat. There were a group of us."

"How long ago was this?" Mark asked.

"About a year ago."

"Who made up the group?" Mark asked.

"A couple of his friends and some people that used to work with him. I believe they were having an impromptu celebration about a major case they had just won."

Mark reached for a legal pad and pen. "Would you be able to give me the names of some of the people on board the boat that night?"

Jones' brow wrinkled in thought as he tried to recall the names of those who were present. "Let's see, there was Evan Millstone and his sister, Sharon. They went sailing with Rick on a fairly frequent basis. Then there was his secretary, Marissa."

"Marissa James was on board?" Mark questioned, recalling the woman's comments about never being able to make it out of the marina due to seasickness.

"Yes, she was. But to be honest, I'm not quite sure just how often she sailed. She looked a little green around the gills."

"But she did go sailing that night?" Mark persisted.

"Yes, she managed to make it without incident."

Mark's eyes met Walt's across the desk in silent communication before he shifted his attention back to Benjamin. "Do you remember any names of other people present?"

"Brooke Jennings was there."

"Did you have a lot of communication with Brooke in the past? Other than this instance?" Mark questioned.

"I wouldn't say a lot. I frequently saw her around. As I mentioned, my boat was docked two slips down from Rick's, and I did live in the same building as the man."

"Just out of curiosity, how did you come to be invited to the impromptu party?" Walt asked.

"Rick was in a good mood that night. I think he just wanted to celebrate with people. I'm not sure it mattered who they were."

"Is there anything else?" Mark asked, jotting down a note.

"No. I just thought you should be aware of what I saw."

Mark thought about the information they had just

learned. "We appreciate you taking the time to come down and talk to us," he said. Reaching for his business card, he held it out across the desk. "If you can think of anything else that you believe we might find useful, or if you notice anybody hanging around Cory's boat, please call me."

Jones took the card and glanced at it before placing it inside his wallet. "I will."

"Are you sure there's not anything else that you'd like to say right now?" Walt asked.

"I can't think of anything."

"But just to clarify, you never actually saw Brooke Jennings. You only heard her," Mark said.

Jones glanced over at him. "That's right."

Mark nodded. "You've been very helpful. And you have my card. If you can think of anything else, please be sure to call me day or night."

"I will." Jones stood to leave.

"Detective Tyler will see you out," Mark said, watching as they left the room.

It was only a couple of minutes before Walt returned. He sat in the same seat.

"Well?" Walt asked.

Mark leaned back and tapped a pen against the legal pad on his desktop. "I'm not sure how much help the man was."

"I know. I was hoping that he would give us something tangible to work with. But it was only speculation."

"He said Brooke was on the boat a couple of weeks ago, but he never actually saw her face. And regardless of what the man says, I seriously doubt he had enough interaction with Brooke to recognize her voice from an enclosed space while she was walking by."

"Yeah. That bothered me too."

"That doesn't mean it didn't happen, it's just not something I'm willing to say with one hundred percent certainty."

"And then there's the fact that the man claimed Marissa James was on board the boat, when she just told us today that she gets seasick."

"His assertion was at total odds with her statement. And she did make the comment about only recently being invited on the boat. The cruise Benjamin Jones was talking about happened over a year ago. That's in direct conflict of what she told us," Mark said.

"It could just be that was the only occasion she was out on the boat. Maybe the incident Benjamin Jones referred to slipped her mind," Walt suggested.

"I don't buy that."

"So how do you want to proceed from here?"

"I'll try and talk to Brooke again tonight to see if she can shed any light on what Jones just said."

"She never mentioned being on Rick Cory's boat a couple of weeks ago?" Walt asked.

"No. She admitted running into him a couple of weeks ago, but she said it was at the bank."

"Maybe after running into each other, they made arrangements to meet on his sailboat later in the evening."

"Possibly. But somehow I get the impression that Brooke would have mentioned that to me."

"But you can't be sure of that."

Mark expelled a breath. "Right now, I can't be sure of anything," he said, reaching once again for the report on the earring. "I was hoping that there might have been a small amount of trace evidence on the post of the earring. That would have at least given us something to work with."

"Even if there was, it might have been irrelevant. With the exception of the strand of hair found in Cory's watch strap, we don't have any samples to compare it to."

Mark grunted and turned his attention to the notes he had written on Benjamin Jones. "With any luck, Brooke will fill in some blanks tonight."

"Call me if you find out anything."

"I will."

Chapter Eighteen

An hour later, Mark parked in his driveway. As he shut the engine, he glanced over at Brooke's house, surprised to see her bent over her flower garden, weeding. Dusk had already fallen, and her security lights illuminated her actions. He watched her pull up weeds, her actions slow and methodic.

Opening his car door, he stepped out and studied her over the hood. "Brooke?"

Brooke jumped slightly at the sound of her name. Turning in Mark's direction, she smiled. "Mark. Hi."

Mark closed his car door. "Hi," he said, his eyes going down to her flower bed. "It's kind of late to be doing that, isn't it?"

Brooke shrugged. "I needed to do something to work off some excess energy."

"One of those type of days?"

"One of those. You're home kind of late."

"Something came up."

149

Brooke dropped her gardening tools and walked over to the hedges that separated their properties. "About the murder?"

"Yeah," he said, his hands motioning to the dirt marks on her shorts. "You're never going to be able to get those stains out."

Brooke followed his gaze, grimacing as she noticed the mess she had made of her clothes. "I guess it's a good thing that they're old."

"Hmm," he said before looking into her eyes. "Do you have a few moments? I'd like to talk to you again about Rick."

"Of course. Shall we do it over dinner?"

"Sounds good. Just give me a few minutes to wash up."

She looked down at her own hands. "I need some time to get myself cleaned up too."

Mark glanced at his watch. "Thirty minutes?"

"Perfect."

"I'll see you then."

Later, Mark sat out on the patio with Brooke. Dinner was done, the grill cleaned and put away.

"So, what did you want to know about Rick?" she asked as she poured coffee for the both of them.

Mark stared at her for a moment, debating on how to start the conversation. He needed to talk to her about what Benjamin Jones said. He needed to find out from her whether or not she had more of a reunion with Rick a few weeks ago than she had originally let on. He knew that the best way to find out the information was to come right out and ask, to not give her a hint beforehand of the information he was after. Her reaction to

his words could very well give him the answer he needed. He didn't want to blind-side her, but he did need to
know the truth. He hesitated only a moment before saying, "One of Rick's neighbors paid Walt and myself a
visit today."

"Who?"

"Benjamin Jones. Do you know him?" he asked,
watching her facial expression closely, trying to determine if the name meant anything to her.

"Benjamin Jones?"

"Yes."

"The name sounds familiar, but I'm having a little
trouble placing him. What does he look like?"

Mark shrugged. "He's about five-feet-eight, late
fifties, black hair liberally streaked with gray. He said
his boat is docked two slips away from Rick's. Does the
description ring a bell?"

"I think I know who he is. He came to see you
today?"

"Yes."

"What did he want?"

"He made a comment that he thought you were on
Rick's boat a couple of weeks ago. I need to know if
that's true."

"I was nowhere near Rick's boat," she replied without hesitation.

"Are you sure about that?"

"Positive," she replied, taking a sip from her coffee.
"Did he actually say that he saw me?"

"No. Like I said, he only thought you were near the
boat. He didn't actually see you."

"What made him think it was me?"

"Apparently, he thought he recognized your voice."

Brooke contemplated Mark's words. "Considering that any association I had with the man was minimal, I don't know what makes him think that he knows the sound of my voice."

"That's one of the reasons that I wanted to have you confirm if what he was saying was true. I wasn't sure how well you knew the man."

"I don't know him well at all. The only thing I do know is that he was mistaken about who was on Rick's boat."

Mark nodded. "But you did see Rick a few weeks ago?" he asked, thinking back to their original conversation the day the body had been discovered floating in the surf.

"Yes, but like I told you earlier, it was only at the bank. And it was only briefly."

"That was the only time you saw him recently?"

"The only time," she confirmed, thinking about why Benjamin Jones would have said what he did. "Just out of curiosity, did Benjamin mention why he thought it important to bring this to your attention?"

"I think he was only trying to be helpful. Walt and I were at Rick's apartment building today, trying to find out information that would help with the investigation. Benjamin Jones found out about our visit and called us saying that he might have some information that he thought we would find useful."

"How would this type of information be useful?"

"Just filling in some blanks of who would have had contact with Rick recently could be a great help. It would give us some idea of who we could get information from regarding his death."

"Makes sense."

"I would be negligent if I didn't investigate every lead with a case," Mark said, not wanting to offend her in any way, but keeping in mind that she was still a possible suspect in the murder.

"I know," she acknowledged softly.

Mark offered her a brief smile of gratitude for her understanding, and leaned back in his chair. "The man did mention something else that I wanted to ask you about."

"What's that?"

"He mentioned that Rick threw an impromptu party on his boat right before you two broke up."

"That's right," she said, recalling the evening.

"He said Marissa James was on board the boat. Was that true?"

"Yes, it was. Rick had just won a big court case. It was one of those rare moments that he felt like celebrating in a big way."

"What do you mean by one of those rare moments?"

"Like I mentioned before, Rick was a very private person. He wasn't into impromptu parties."

"But he was on that night."

"Yes. Why?"

"Walt and I spoke to Marissa James today."

"So?"

"So, she claimed that it was only recently that she was invited onto Rick's boat. She made it sound like Rick had never asked her to go sailing with him before."

Brooke tapped her fingernails against the glass top of the table as she considered Mark's words. "I know that's not true. I know for a fact that Rick had invited her to go with us on a couple of different occasions."

"Did she ever take him up on the offer?"

"No, but I know he did ask."

"Do you have any idea of why she didn't go?"

"Yes. Marissa's worst enemy seems to be the water. She gets seasick very quickly."

"But she didn't the night of the party?" he asked, trying to get clarification on whether Marissa had been truthful that afternoon. He knew the incongruities between Brooke's words and those of Marissa could just be a difference in how something was perceived.

"No, she managed to survive. But just barely. To be honest, she was a little out of it that night. She spent a good portion of the evening sleeping in the cabin below."

"Benjamin Jones failed to mention that part."

"That doesn't surprise me."

"Why do you say that?"

"There's something else that I think Benjamin failed to mention to you about that night."

"What?"

"Benjamin spent most of the night trying to get Rick to go into a partnership."

"Partnership? With what?"

"With his daughter."

Mark's eyes narrowed slightly at her words. "I don't understand. What kind of partnership did he want Rick to have with his daughter?"

"Benjamin's daughter is also an attorney."

"So?"

"So, she had gone up against Rick several times in the courtroom. She was very impressed with his style."

"And she wanted to open a practice together," Mark concluded.

"Exactly."

"What's Benjamin's daughter's name?"

"Rachel Jones."

Mark nodded, making a mental note of the name so that he could run a background check on the woman. "Why was Benjamin involved? What would he have stood to gain by coercing Rick into a possible partnership with his daughter?"

"I'm not sure. All I know for certain was that Rick wasn't interested in taking on any partners."

"Did he make that clear to Benjamin?" Mark asked, getting a clear picture that Benjamin Jones' willingness to help the authorities with Cory's murder investigation wasn't necessarily without personal gain. He began to wonder if there might be more of a motive for Benjamin to have contacted Walt today than just that of a good samaritan. He began to wonder if the man was possibly trying to protect his daughter.

"He did."

"What do you think would be the motivation for Benjamin to involve himself in trying to get Rick to change his mind?"

"I can't say for sure, but I got the distinct impression that Rachel was definitely 'daddy's' girl. I'm quite sure that she saw Benjamin's close proximity to Rick as an opportunity to push her advantage to try and get Rick to change his mind."

"Close proximity? What does that mean? That Benjamin Jones and Rick Cory were close friends?"

Brooke shook her head. "Hardly. They were barely acquaintances. They didn't see each other on a regular basis, regardless of the fact that their boats were docked closely to one another, and they lived in the same building. Rick liked to sail in the evening, Benjamin liked to do it strictly on weekends. I think Rachel was hoping they were closer though. At least close enough to give her father some leverage in changing Rick's mind."

"So the chances of Benjamin Jones and Rick running into each other on a regular basis would have been slim."

"That's right."

"And that night the entire group went sailing wasn't an everyday occurrence, or even a weekly one."

"Right again."

"So the question remains, why was Benjamin trying to give us the impression that he had a closer relationship with Rick than he actually did."

"I have no idea. I can count on one hand the amount of times I ran into Benjamin Jones while with Rick. And other than that night when we all went sailing, I'm trying to figure out when I had a long enough conversation with the man where he would have been able to recognize my voice without actually seeing me."

"That is a little strange," Mark admitted, wondering if Brooke was being entirely truthful with him in how often she actually saw the man.

"It's more than a little strange."

"If what you're saying is true, it'll be interesting to see what we'll be able to find out about the man and his daughter. Maybe there's more here than meets the eye."

Chapter Nineteen

The following morning, Mark was just finishing a final cup of coffee when his doorbell rang. He glanced at his watch. It wasn't even seven. With a frown, he got up from the sofa to answer its summons.

"Morning," Mark said, his voice betraying his surprise at finding Walt on his doorstep.

"Hi. I'm not interrupting anything, am I?" Walt asked.

Mark frowned. "Of course not. Come in."

"Thanks."

"What's up?"

"The background check we ran on Benjamin Jones came in," Walt said, handing him a file.

"That was quick," Mark said as he automatically flipped open the document.

"Yeah, it was. But I'm going to be the last one to complain about it."

"You've been to the station already?"

"I couldn't sleep, so I went down to the station to get caught up on some paperwork. While I was there, the report came in. After reading it, I thought you would want to see it."

Mark nodded. "Thanks."

"Don't mention it."

"Anything interesting?"

"Read it for yourself," Walt said, a sense of satisfaction in his voice.

Mark raised an eyebrow at his words and turned his attention to the report. "Benjamin Jones was in debt. That's nothing unusual. That would apply to most of the population."

"He was in serious debt though. The kind of debt that could crucify a life."

Mark shrugged. "That doesn't connect him to Cory's murder."

"It does if he was looking for Cory's help to rectify his situation."

Mark grunted. "According to this, Benjamin Jones was a gambler. A heavy one. Most of his debts were accrued at the dog track."

"Yes. And he had a daughter Rachel who used to bail him out constantly."

Mark frowned as his eyes caught note of something in the document. "It says here that Rachel Jones took a second mortgage out on her house to pay off her father's debt."

"Yep. Keep reading. I think you'll be pleasantly surprised."

Mark continued to scan the report. "Her law practice was in trouble due to the financial burden."

"That's right. Just out of curiosity, did you get a chance to talk to Brooke about Benjamin Jones' visit?"

"I talked to her yesterday after I got home. She told me that Rachel Jones was interested in going into partnership with Rick Cory."

"Maybe to help her out financially. Sharing an office space, sharing business expenses, would have probably helped a lot."

"Yeah, it would."

Walt walked into the kitchen and over to the fridge. Opening the door, he lifted out a can of soda. "May I?"

"Help yourself," Mark said as he took the file back to the sofa he had been sitting on, and reached for his own cup of coffee.

Walt popped the top and took a deep drink before wiping the back of his hand across his mouth. "So what do you think?"

"I think we need to investigate Benjamin Jones and his daughter Rachel a little bit more."

"I agree. So now the question is, where do we start?"

Mark leaned back, propping his feet up on the coffee table. "I think the first thing we need to do is go and talk to his daughter. We have her address. I think we should make an unannounced visit."

"Do you think she may be involved in this mess?"

"I don't know. I think it's interesting that she wanted something from Rick Cory that he was unwilling to give her."

"It's a long shot that it would be the motive for his death."

"We don't have much else to go on right now."

"That's true," Walt said, absently glancing out the window. "Your neighbor gets up pretty early, huh."

"What?"

"Your neighbor. She's a morning person."

"Brooke?"

"That would be the one."

Mark shook his head. "You must be mistaken. Brooke moves in slow motion in the morning," he said, thinking of all the times during the school year that he saw her practically shuffling out to her car.

"Not today. She's getting in her car."

"Are you sure?" Mark asked as he got to his feet to see if what Walt was saying was true.

"You could have just taken my word on it. There was no need to check for yourself," Walt said with a laugh.

Mark didn't respond to his humor. "Come on."

"Where are we going?"

"I want to follow her," Mark said, not offering any further explanation as he headed toward the door. He wanted to get to his car before she got too far of a head start. He wanted to know where she was going. He remembered their conversation the night before regarding Benjamin Jones' comment about thinking that Brooke had been on Rick's boat a few weeks before his murder. He couldn't help but wonder if her leaving her house this early had something to do with that conversation.

"Do you mind if I ask why?"

"Does it matter why?" Mark returned, as he locked the door behind him and walked to his car. "Come on, I'll drive."

Ten minutes later, Mark and Walt sat in the car by a

curb, watching from a safe distance as Brooke drove her car into the marina where Cory's boat was docked. Traffic was light that morning in the marina, only a few cars dotted the gravel lot, and she had no trouble securing a parking space.

"What do you think she's doing here?" Walt asked, watching as Brooke turned her head to scan the immediate area, as if searching for something. A full minute passed before she cut her engine and opened her car door.

"I'm not sure. She made the comment yesterday that Benjamin Jones sailed on the weekends. Today's Saturday. Maybe she came to pay the man a visit."

"Or maybe she came because Cory's boat is docked here," Walt suggested.

"Maybe. Either way, we're about to find out."

Mark and Walt watched Brooke leave her car and walk toward the floating dock that led to *Cory's Pleasure* and Benjamin Jones' boat.

Mark waited long enough for Brooke to clear the area, not wanting her to suspect that they were following her. Once he was satisfied that she was a safe distance away, his hand went to his door handle. "Let's go."

Mark and Walt followed a respectable distance away from Brooke, being careful to stay out of her line of vision. They watched as she stopped in front of Cory's sailboat.

"She's definitely going to *Cory's Pleasure,*" Walt said as she easily moved between the police tape that secured the area.

Mark watched her step lithely on the boat. He noticed

that she glanced around the area before moving to the hatch, and he tried to come to terms with what he was seeing. There was only one reason that he could think of for Brooke to come back to the marina, for her to come back to the scene of the crime. She had to be involved in the murder. The thought hit him hard. He couldn't believe that he had been so wrong about her. He couldn't believe that his instincts had been so off. He couldn't help but think that maybe Benjamin Jones had been right when he said he heard Brooke with Rick a few weeks before his death. Maybe their conversation last night regarding the man's words triggered something in her subconscious. Something that she needed to put to rest

"Aren't you going to stop her?" Walt asked.

"No."

"Why not?"

Mark glanced at him, his eyes hard. "I want her to get caught in her own web," he said, feeling a sense of betrayal from her actions. He had trusted her. He had considered her a friend. When Walt had been ready to cast her as a suspect earlier in the investigation, he had been the one to defend her. Watching her now, he felt as if he had been deceived. She moved around the crime scene without a care, as if she had done it before. Which if he thought about the situation logically, is exactly what had happened.

"But—"

"Relax. She's not going to do any harm. We have all of the evidence from on board. Let her roam a little bit. Let her get her fingerprints all over the place. It'll give us more evidence in court."

"You want her to hang," Walt said.

"More than you know."

"Mark," Walt began, wanting to try and reason with him.

"Don't say anything, Walt." Mark moved swiftly to the boat, his steps light and soundless.

Walt sighed. He didn't like to see Mark like this. He didn't like that Brooke was the cause. He had always known that Mark could be ruthless. In his profession he had to be. But seeing him now, as he stalked after Brooke, caused the hair on his neck to stand on end. He had never seen anyone so angry. Mark looked as if one wrong word was going to send him over the edge. Walt just prayed that Brooke didn't utter that word. Realizing that he had better follow after him just to ensure that nobody got caught in any crossfire, he forced himself to move.

Mark watched as Brooke struggled with the hatch for a moment before climbing down the ladder to the cabin below. He quickly followed suit.

As he neared the companionway, he heard voices raised in anger, and he automatically paused. Brooke had met someone here. It was something that he hadn't expected.

Listening intently, he realized that there was something vaguely familiar about the voice of the person with Brooke. An inflection in the tone that he recognized. Mark knew instinctively that the person with Brooke was someone he knew.

He took a step forward, being careful not to alert anybody to his presence. He wasn't sure what he was about to walk into, and he knew he couldn't afford not to have the upper hand. He heard Brooke speak again before he heard the harsh response from the person with her, and it was that response that enabled him to identify the owner of the voice. It was Megan Smith.

The shock of hearing Megan's voice stopped Mark cold. He knew she wasn't authorized to be on the boat. Nobody was. At least not without clearance. Which was something he knew Megan had not been granted. There was no reason for her to have been given permission to board the vessel. The previous searches had been completed.

Suspicion swept through him. Megan's presence on the boat just didn't make sense. She was too professional to go against orders. She would never do anything to contaminate a crime scene. She would never do anything that would ruin the integrity of a case. He knew with clear certainty that Megan had to have her own reasons to come to the boat. Reasons that had nothing to do with her job. Reasons that somehow tied her to Cory's murder.

He heard both Brooke and Megan speak again, and he was stunned by the fury evident in Megan's words, in her tone of voice. It was a rage so palpable, and so out of character with Mark's perception of her that it immediately triggered flashbacks of the two crucial pieces of evidence uncovered in Cory's murder investigation: The strand of hair that Walt had found on the victim that by Megan's own words matched hers, and the earring found on the boat and Megan's initial excitement as she laid claim to it. Excitement that had faded after she learned where the earring had been discovered. Mark had a sudden insight into why. In that moment, he saw clearly what he should have seen all along. Megan killed Cory.

The clues of her involvement in the murder were there for anybody who wanted to see them. They were there for anybody who was willing to believe that somebody who took an oath to uphold the law would use their position as a shield to hide their actions. The way the boat had been cleaned after the murder, and the lack of evidence present on board the boat were testaments to just how good Megan was at her job. Of her in-depth knowledge of what she had to accomplish if she was literally going to get away with murder. Of what she needed to do to manipulate the evidence so that nothing pointed in her direction.

Suddenly, her constant early arrivals and late departures at the police precinct made sense. Her willingness to go above and beyond the call of duty in processing the evidence gave her the leverage and isolation she needed to effectively alter any results on the evidence collected, so that none of it would point in her direction. But even as Mark became aware of what he had been blind to, he knew there were still several unanswered questions. Why had Megan murdered Cory? What was her motive? And what was Brooke doing on the boat? Was it possible that Brooke was an accomplice? He had never heard either of them mention one another's name, but he was starkly aware that both of them seemed to have secrets. Both of them seemed to have their own agenda. Their presence on the boat was proof of that.

Pulling his gun from his holster, he edged toward the

opening of the companionway. He didn't look back to see if Walt was following him. It was immaterial. He was going in with or without backup.

He stepped down the ladder, his eyes trying to adjust to the dimness of the cabin. He saw the two shadowy figures, and he glanced at their hands, trying to determine if they were armed. Unable to see anything in the darkness, he trained his gun on his targets. Two people together were harder to cover than one, but the tightness of the cabin ensured that he would be able to manage it. Taking a deep breath, he barked, "Megan! Brooke!"

Chapter Twenty

"She has a gun, Mark!" Brooke shouted, coming out of the shadows.

Mark heard the fear in her voice, and his eyes went to Megan's hand, seeing the small caliber gun. "Drop it!" he ordered.

"I don't think so," Megan said, her hand beginning to shake at the situation she found herself in.

"You pull the trigger on that gun, and you won't leave the boat alive," he promised, seeing the desperation in her eyes, in her actions. Knowing that the situation was volatile, he never broke eye contact with her. He couldn't afford to give her any edge in dictating how this whole scenario was going to play out. He held out a hand to her. "Give me the gun, Megan."

She shook her head. "No."

"You don't want to do anything rash," Mark said, trying to reason with her, trying to get her to drop her guard.

"Let me go, and there won't be any problems."

"I can't do that," Mark said as he took a step closer to her.

Megan took a step back, keeping her gun trained on Brooke. "Take one more step, and she's history."

Mark stopped dead in his tracks, seeing the slight trembling of her finger on the trigger. One wrong twitch and the gun would go off. "All right, take it easy. There's no reason for anyone to get hurt."

"I mean it," she ground out angrily.

"I believe you," Mark said her, all the while wondering where Walt was.

"Good," she muttered, taking another step backward until her back was against the wall.

Mark watched her movements carefully. All of his instincts told him to take her out of the picture, but Brooke was standing too close to her. He couldn't take the chance that she would be injured. He glanced briefly at Brooke. "Are you okay?" he asked, not understanding what Brooke was doing on the boat, but unwilling to debate the situation with her now. His only concern at the moment was to get them both off the boat alive. Then he would give her ample opportunity to explain her actions.

Brooke looked at him, drawing strength from the steely determination visible in his eyes, in his body language. "Yes."

Mark nodded, and immediately turned his attention back to Megan. He noticed she was still shaking. Her obvious lack of control over her emotions was what caused the situation to be so dangerous, so near exploding. "Why did you kill Rick Cory?" he asked, wondering if his words would have enough of a shock effect to give him the upper hand in the situation. He wasn't quite sure if Megan fully understood that there was no way out for her. That for all intents and purposes, she couldn't walk away from the predicament she had gotten herself into. Watching the expressions cross her face, he knew the exact moment his words registered. It was when her attention focused on him, rather than Brooke.

"What?" Megan asked, full fledged panic noticeable in her gaze and in her voice.

"I know you killed Rick," Mark said, keeping his voice even and calm. "I want to know why. What did he do to you that justified you taking his life?" he asked, his tone of voice almost conversational. Almost, but not entirely. There was an edge present that warned anybody who knew him that they were skating on thin ice.

Megan quickly regained her composure and glared at Mark. She didn't even bother to deny his words. "Rick deserved to die," she hissed.

"Why? What possible reason could you have to want to kill him?" Mark took a tiny step closer, only to stop as she lifted the gun.

"Don't," she warned.

Mark did as she directed, not ready to test her mindset. He needed to try and reason with her first. "Talk to me Megan. Tell me why Rick deserved to die." He wanted to be able to intercept her if she even thought about pulling the trigger. Her demeanor was too shaky, too much on edge. There seemed to be an irrational momentum about her movements, and he didn't trust that he was going to be able to talk her out of the path of madness that she seemed bent on taking. He knew his best bet to get Brooke out safely rested with his ability to read the woman's intentions before she had a chance to carry them out.

"Why?"

"Why not?" he countered, all of his concentration on the woman who virtually held Brooke hostage. "Tell me why you're here," he said, trying to keep his voice non-threatening.

When she didn't respond to his comment, he pushed her a little bit more. "Talk to me, Megan. Let me try and help you. Tell me why you killed Rick Cory."

Megan's eyes wavered between Mark and Brooke, and she gripped her gun harder. "Rick deserved to die," she repeated, sidestepping his question entirely.

"Why?"

"What's it to you?"

Mark shrugged. "I want to help you. I thought we were friends. You know you're not going to walk out of here. Explain to me what happened, and it might change your situation."

"Why should I trust you?"

"Because I'm telling you that you can."

Megan shook her head. "That's not a good enough reason for me to take you at your word."

"What are your other options?"

She shrugged, not responding to his words.

Mark tried again. "Help me to understand why you killed Rick Cory."

She took a deep breath. "It doesn't matter why. It's too late to change the situation."

"You and I both know it's never to late. Talk to me, Megan. Help me to help you."

There was a long pause. "Rick defended my mother's assailant," she finally said, her voice barely above a whisper.

Understanding dawned for Mark. "He's the lawyer who got the guy acquitted." He knew from past conversations with her that her mother was never the same after the attack. He knew her mother had been in deep depression for a long time. He suddenly recalled an instance several months back when Megan had taken personal leave so that she could get her mother settled in another state with her sister. The woman had gone so far downhill that she required constant care.

Megan's eyes shimmered with unshed tears. "You know my mother suffered after that attack. Her personality changed. She became just a shell of her old self."

"I know. And because of your mother's deteriorating health, you wanted revenge."

"I wanted justice!" she corrected. "The man who assaulted my mother should never have walked. He confessed to the crime. Rick was the one who got him to recant the confession. If the man would have been convicted, my mother might have felt some sort of closure. She might have been able to deal with what had happened."

"You're putting a lot of faith into speculation. Your mother got a raw deal. There's no denying that. And I'm sorry that it happened. But killing Rick Cory wasn't the answer. Rick didn't attack your mother."

"He's guilty by association!"

At her words, Mark knew that there would be no reasoning with her. Her thinking was skewed. She was no longer in touch with reality. He didn't know if the reason was because she felt cornered, or if it was something else. He tried a different tactic. "What was your reason for coming back to the boat today?" Mark asked, noticing that she was beginning to let down her guard slightly. He took a tentative step forward.

"Don't do it," she warned.

Mark immediately stopped. "Why did you come back here? What is it that you're looking for?"

"What I'm doing here doesn't concern you."

Mark didn't respond to her words, instead he glanced around the room, looking for an explanation for her presence on the boat. He froze when he spotted the small can of gasoline resting in the corner. His eyes shot up in disbelief. "You were going to torch the boat?"

"What do you mean 'were?'"

Mark shook his head. "Why?"

"Because I can't stop thinking about that night. I want this place destroyed," she shot back.

"It won't change the outcome of anything by setting fire to this boat."

Megan shrugged. "Maybe not. But it'll sure give me a lot of personal satisfaction. Rick loved this boat. It'll give me great pleasure to destroy it. I should have done it the night I killed him. I would have saved myself a lot of aggravation." She turned to look at Brooke. "Why did you come here today? Now you're going to have to be part of this," she muttered as she trained her gun on Brooke and reached down to knock over the gasoline can. The smell of the fumes instantly flooded the cabin.

"What are you doing?" Brooke asked, panic lending an edge to her voice.

Megan reached into her pants pocket and removed a lighter. "What does it look like?" She backed up toward the hatch to make her escape.

"But you can't do that," Brooke said angrily.

"Watch me," she said as her thumb flicked the little switch that caused the flame to appear.

The moment he saw the flame, Mark knew the time for talking had ended. Without a thought, his arm snaked out to pull Brooke behind his body just as he raised his gun to fire.

Megan, angry at the move, screeched with rage. Grabbing her gun with both hands, she released her grip on the lighter, causing it to drop harmlessly to the ground.

Mark watched the panic in her eyes, and tried once more to reason with her to drop the gun. The cabin was small, and with the gasoline already pooled on the floor, there was too great a chance of the whole boat exploding should either of them fire. His eyes caught a slight movement behind her, only the briefest of shadows, but he knew instinctively that Walt was now in the small enclosed area. "Drop your weapon!"

Megan shook her head at his order, and her finger went to the trigger. Her whole body was shaking with emotion as she took aim. "No!"

"Walt!" Mark shouted, his eyes looking past Megan.

Megan turned blindly to see who was behind her.

The moment she did, Mark rushed and grabbed her. She struggled wildly within his grasp, both his hand and hers struggling for control of her weapon. Managing to get her throat in a stranglehold, he pried the gun from her hand, watching as it fell to the ground. He quickly kicked it in Walt's direction.

Walt reached for the gun and lifted it. "I have it," he said before turning to look at Mark and Brooke. "You both okay?"

Mark nodded, but didn't release his grip on his captive. "Yeah. Hand me your cuffs, will you?"

Mark shifted his hold on Megan just enough to allow him to bring both of her arms behind her back. He quickly cuffed her. "What took you so long to get here?" he asked Walt.

"There were a couple of curious bystanders outside. I had to make sure they cleared the area."

Mark nodded and turned to look at Brooke. He was slightly startled to see the paleness of her features. Handing Megan over to Walt, he walked back to Brooke. "Are you okay?"

Brooke crossed her arms and nodded. "I'm fine."

Mark studied her in silence. Her demeanor and slight trembling were totally at odds with her words. Without a second thought, he reached out and pulled her into his arms, holding her tightly. "It's okay, you know. I won't let anybody or anything hurt you."

Brooke closed her eyes as she leaned into his strength. "I know you wouldn't."

"So why are you shaking?"

"I don't know."

"Everything's going to be all right."

Brooke nodded slightly before looking over at Megan. "What's going to happen to her?"

Mark shrugged. "That's for the District Attorney to decide."

"She needs help."

Mark nodded. "I know."

"Mark?"

"Yeah?"

"Thanks."

Chapter Twenty-one

Three hours later, Mark escorted Brooke home. She had already given her statement down at the police station, and Megan had been booked for the murder of Rick Cory.

"How are you holding up?" he asked.

"I'm fine," she assured him as she petted an enthusiastic Jake. "I'm having a little trouble coming to terms with everything, but other than that, I'm fine."

"It's a lot to come to terms with."

"I know. I can't believe she killed Rick because he did his job," she said for what seemed like the hundredth time.

"There's a lot of things in life that don't make sense. Megan's mother was never the same after she was assaulted. I don't think anybody truly had any idea of just how much that incident impacted her life, or Megan's for that matter. Nobody could have guessed that Megan held Cory responsible. That she would go after him to avenge the situation."

"But Megan worked with you, Mark. How could she be capable of committing murder?"

"Honey, everybody's capable of it given the right circumstances. And anybody that tells you differently is just fooling themselves."

Brooke was silent for a moment. "But cold-blooded murder?"

"This wasn't cold-blooded, not by a long shot. Rick's murder was definitely premeditated. Megan had the whole thing planned out down to the last detail."

"But she worked for the police."

"Maybe that was where she got the idea that she could kill Rick and get away with it. Nobody would know more than Megan just what type of evidence you would have to clean up from a crime scene to ensure that the crime couldn't be traced. She knew exactly what to do and what not to do."

"She needs psychological help."

"She'll get it. You weren't hurt at all, were you?" He had tried to get her to go to the hospital to be checked out, but she was adamant that she was all right.

"No," she assured him before giving Jake one final pat. She stood and walked in the direction of the kitchen. "I'm going to put on a pot of coffee. Join me?"

"Sure." Mark followed her and took a seat at her kitchen table. He watched as she moved confidently around the kitchen. After several moments of comfortable silence, he said, "I need to ask you something."

"Of course."

"Why did you go back to the marina this morning?"

Brooke finished spooning the coffee into the filter before responding to his question. "I wanted to talk to Benjamin Jones. I knew he spent the weekends on his boat. I wanted to know why he felt the need to try and implicate me in Rick's murder. But then I saw someone on Rick's boat and I went to investigate."

"You should have called me immediately."

"I know," she acknowledged, throwing him a look of apology over her shoulder. "I'm sorry I didn't."

Mark heard the sincerity of her words, and his eyes met hers. "If it's any consolation, I don't think Benjamin Jones was trying to implicate you in Rick's murder. I think he was trying to be of help to the authorities. He did hear someone with Rick that night. But he was below deck, and the voices were muffled."

"He probably heard Megan with Rick."

"Probably."

"She was the new relationship Sharon and Evan were referring to," she said, unable to hide her hurt at the thought.

"It looks that way."

She nodded and took a deep breath, trying to get control of her emotions. "I'm sorry I went to the boat. I almost got you killed."

"I was more worried about you. I wish you would have called me."

She looked over at him, her eyes meeting his. "Would you have let me go to the marina to talk to Benjamin?"

He held her gaze for a moment longer before admitting, "No."

She smiled wryly. "That's why I didn't call you."

"Fair enough."

"It never occurred to me that I would run into someone on Rick's boat. I guess that was a little naïve on my part."

"The important thing is that you're safe."

"Thanks to you."

"When I think about what could have happened—"

"Nothing did," she reminded him.

"But it was close. Too close for comfort."

"I know," she acknowledged, falling silent.

"What are you thinking?"

"I can't believe that we found Rick's murderer."

"I'm just glad that we did."

"Why do you think she went back to the boat to set fire to it?"

"She probably was beginning to second guess her actions. Maybe she thought that if the boat was destroyed, the case would disappear. Maybe she realized that she didn't clean up the crime scene as well as she originally thought. The reason doesn't matter. The bottom line is that she was careless. She couldn't stay away from the scene of the crime. It's what caused her downfall today."

Brooke retrieved the cups, keeping her back toward him as she paused by the cabinet. "Tell me something."

"Anything."

She turned to face him. "You were beginning to suspect me, weren't you?"

He shrugged without apology. "There were things that I couldn't make heads or tales of. There seemed to be a lot of evasion coming from you."

"I never really severed my emotional ties with Rick," she admitted as she moved back to the table.

"I know."

Brooke picked up the coffee carafe. After pouring out two mugs, she took a seat opposite him. Reaching out, she touched his hand gently. "I'd like to thank you for everything."

"No thanks are necessary."

"I think there is."

Mark studied her across the table for a moment before saying, "I think if our situations were reversed, you would do the same for me."

"I would."

Mark stared into her eyes, realizing that the conversation was too serious. He wanted her to relax a little bit. He felt that it would help her adjust to the events of the day. "You know what I think?"

"What?"

"I think we should go out by your pool and unwind."

Brooke turned to look out the sliding glass door at the shimmering water. A slight smile teased her mouth. "I thought you didn't like the heat."

"I don't, but for you, I'll bear it," he told her as he stood and offered her his hand. "It looks like there are two lounge chairs out there with our names on them."

Brooke paused for only a moment before putting her hand in his, feeling his fingers squeeze hers reassuringly. "I think you may be right."

"I know I am," he said as he led her out into the bright sunlight. "And just to show you what a nice guy I am, I'll let you pick the place for dinner tonight."

Brooke smiled at him wryly. "You're hungry?"

"Not yet, but I figure after a couple of hours of lazing in the heat, we'll both be ready for some nourishment." He waited until she was situated on her lounge chair before reclining on his own.

Brooke watched as he relaxed fully and closed his eyes. She reached out to touch his hand. "Mark?"

Mark grasped her hand in his, but didn't open his eyes to look at her. "Yeah?"

"You really are a nice man."

Mark sighed. "Brooke?"

"Yeah?"

"You're supposed to be relaxing."

"I am."

"No, you're not," he said, still not looking over at her.

Brooke looked down at their entwined hands. After giving his a slight squeeze, she laid down and closed her eyes. "One of these days, you'll have to learn how to accept a compliment."

Mark smiled slightly at her words, but he didn't respond. After several minutes, he heard the even breathing that indicated she had fallen asleep. Only then did he relax enough to allow himself to drift off, his hand still holding hers.